1

ISBN 0-9716567-6-2
The Gizmo Tales: Hero Dogs
Jeri Fink and Donna Paltrowitz
Book Web Publishing, Ltd.
www.bookwebpublishing.com

Book Cover Design by Jeremy Ryan

How To Order:
Single or bulk copies can be ordered from:
Book Web Publishing, Ltd.
PO Box 81
Bellmore, NY 11710
or online at:
www.bookwebpublishing.com

Visit us online at www.bookwebpublishing.com

The Gizmo Tales: Hero Dogs

by Jeri Fink and Donna Paltrowitz

FUTURECORPS

Meadow Drive Students Create Books for a Cause

WLNY TV 55

Mystery Writers of America
presents
The Edgar Award
2002
presented to

The Lawrence Ledger

Spring, 2002
Date

schools

CLOSEUP

...dog gets his day

Newsday

FUTURECORPS

LI Hebrew Academy Students Recycle To Help The Blind

The writ...

NEWS 12

minneapolis star tribune

Serving the Merricks for over 60 years

MERRICK LIFE

Books By Teens For Teens

We believe that teenagers are the best-equipped people to talk about their lives, worlds, and interests. We publish books by teens for teens, incorporating young people's voices, experiences, insights, and ideas in everything we produce. Through schools across the country, we invite kids to participate in the writing, editing, designing, reviewing, and promoting of their own book. Participants write a personal dedication, and help illustrate the book. Please take a moment to read what the student-authors say about their work.

Thanks for listening to the kids!

Jeri Fink and Donna Paltrowitz

Book Web Publishing, Ltd.

Thank you for making this project possible!

Newsday FUTURECORPS

Bellmore-Merrick
Central High School District

The Gizmo Tales: Hero Dogs

is dedicated to the heroic dogs and people in this book who generously donated their time, knowledge, and experience to show how our canine heroes can be role models for us all.

Special thanks from Jeri and Donna to:

Dr. Walter C. Woolley, who provided the original spark.
Richard Fink, for his superlative photography and
commitment to Book Web.

Bendzlowicz Family for sharing "Wimpy" and their family history.
Darren Paltrowitz, for his novel approach to thinking and editing.
David Fink for sharing his observations from the Middle East.
Gizmo, for being our favorite labradoodle and
Coco for being his "sister."
Jeremy Ryan, for his amazing artistry and technical advice.
Russell Fink, for his creative consultations.
Roberta "Bunny" Chapman, for her hard work and patience.
Stacey Rossi, for sharing her knowledge of books and publishing.
Shari Paltrowitz, for being our number one "reader."

Borders Bookstore in Westbury, New York for welcoming
Merrick Avenue Middle School student-authors.

To our husbands, Rick and Stuart, and the young people in our
lives, David, Russell, Ann, Meryl, Tony, Stacey, Greg, Adam,
Yvonne, Darren, Aiko, and Shari who share the optimism and vision
of their generation.

To the special seniors in our lives, Larry Milman, Sylvia Gelernter,
Harvey and Edna Fink, Robin March, and Herbert Michelson, who
leaped generations to join us in The Gizmo Tales: Hero Dogs.

To our families and friends who share in all of Gizmo's Tales.
Thanks for your support!

In loving memory of Gladys Milman, Joseph March, Ruth Roth,
Judy Becker, Dora Eisenstein, and Persis Burlingame.

I am so lucky to be in a profession that affords me the talent and challenges of working with young students. Their minds are always open sponges looking to soak up as much information as possible. Learning seems to be second nature to most of them, and a challenge is always met with honest pursuit. These students were given the task of creating a nonfiction book, and they put their minds to work and their pens to paper. I am so proud of their thoughts and ideas that went into the making of **The Gizmo Tales: Hero Dogs.**

Ellen Schwartz

Dedications from the Student-Authors

Adam Brollosy	I dedicate this book to my mom, my dad, Leila, Tamer, Mona, Amira and Noha.
Adam Weingarten	To my great family and awesome friends.
Alex Kantor	I dedicate this to all my family members. I would also like to dedicate this book to Mrs. Schwartz for making this all possible.
Alex Kushner	I dedicate the book to my mom, friends and family and my pet cat named Snowball.
Alex Mendelson	To my mom and dad.
Allie Aucoin	I dedicate this book to my friends and family who have always been there for me.
Aly Vanderwalde	I would like to dedicate this book to all of my family and friends for always being there for me and pushing me to go all the way.
Alyssa De Monte	I dedicate this book to my mom, my dad and my brother who have always been there to keep me going by encouraging me to read and write every day.
Alyssa Goldberg	To my mom, dad, brother and my pets and to the rest of my family and friends.
Alyssa Slater	I dedicate this to my family and friends.
Amanda Cordiello	I dedicate this book to my sister Nicole, my mom and Angelo, my dad and Lynn, and to Mrs. Schwartz for making this book happen. To the Joyce family, the Kaider family, the Ledenko family, the Saffioti family, the Cordiello family, Lorusso family. To my grandparents in Florida and Las Vegas, and to Barbara
Amanda M. D'Archangelis	I dedicate this to my family, all my friends at MAMS and my own dog Buttercup.
Andrew Gitin	I dedicate this book to the tsunami victims and to my family.

Anthony Jon Reyes	I dedicate this to my parents for the support and help through the years.
Anthony Sacco	I would like to thank all my family members and all my friends for the greatest lifetime experiences anyone could ask for.
Ariel Coopersmith	I dedicate this book to my family, friends and Goliath.
Ashley Moran	I dedicate this book to my mom.
Ashley Smith	I would like to dedicate this to my family and friends for always being there for me.
Benjamin Bertan	To Molly for being the only dog in my family.To my supportive family and my great English teacher.
Benjamin Wald	To my supportive family and my great English teacher.
Billy Kuschner	To my grandfather who passed away.
Bobby Iorizzo	To my family, friends and teachers who have helped me get this far and succeed in my life.
Brandon Piskin	Thank you mom, dad, Alex, Jake and my three dogs, Buster, Boomer and Chester.
Brandon Smith	I dedicate this book to my best friends Jake and Ryan and my family.
Brian Demmett	To my dad who loves dogs.
Brian Smith	I dedicate this book to everyone who helped make it.
Briana Grace Cangemi	To my friends and family that I love, thanks for always being there.
Brittany Sacks	I dedicate this book to my family. I love you!
C.J. DiMaggio	To my friends and family.
Caitlan O'Shea	I dedicate this book to my friends, family and my dog Pebbles.
Carla Scolieri	I dedicate this to my family and friends.
Chris Nazario	To my caring family and to all the people who died in 9-11 and the Holocaust.
Christian Stella	To my loving family and friends.

Christina Strezenec	I dedicate this book to the Nassau County Kings and the Rangers sled hockey team, especially Jack. You guys are the best people I've ever met.
Christine Sci	I want to dedicate this book to my family and all my friends.
Claire Tucci	To my friends, family, dogs and cats, who mean a lot to me.
Cory Traustason	I would like to dedicate this book to my golden retriever, Jasmine.
Craig Davide	I dedicate this to my family and friends for helping me get to where I am today.
Danny Daneshgar	To my dedicated parents and my awesome brothers.
Danny Reisner	I dedicate this book to my family and to my dog Gretzky, also to the heroes in the US military and their families.
Dayna Wolf	To my friends and family.
Dean Simms-Elias	I would like to dedicate this book to all of my friends and family.
Deanna Werthauer	To my little fish, Juicy and Saphire and to all the trees that were used to make this book, and to my cousin Maria because she always makes me smile and laugh, thank you!
Denise Tagariello	To my family because they've always been here for me.
Douglas Ryniker	This book is dedicated to my family for always being there for me.
Emily Bernstein	I would like to dedicate this book to my family because they have always been by my side and support me in everything I do.
Eric X. Catafago	I dedicate this to my friends and family.
Eugene Ciniglio	To my friends and family who are there for me.
Francesca Angelini	I dedicate this book to my Nana Sylvia who always took care of dogs all her life.
Frankie Azzara	To all my friends and family.

Gabriella Long	I am dedicating this book to my friends and family.
Heather Segal	I would like to dedicate this book to all of my family, friends and especially Mrs. Schwartz for being such a great teacher and helping me the whole way through!
Heather Swersky	I would like to dedicate this book to my family, friends and all of my teachers who have had a great impact on my life.
Jacqueline Williams	I would like to dedicate this book to my family and friends.
James Levine	I would like to dedicate this book to my huge family and all my friends.
James Raheb	I dedicate this book to my mom, dad, sister and all my friends.
Jennifer Kotler	To my family and friends, you mean the world to me!
Jessica Jaffe	To my family and friends. Also to my brother who had a very hard time this year.
Jessica Peluso	To my mother Marie, my father Ed, my sister Elana and to the rest of my family and friends. Also to all of my past, present and future teachers, especially Mrs. Schwartz, a wonderful English teacher who taught me more about English than I have ever known before this year. Thank you!
Jessica Pollock	I dedicate this to all my family and friends.
Jessica Teves	I dedicate this book to my mom, dad and my sister Katie.
Jimmy Goodheart	I dedicate this book to my family, Theresa, Bernadette, Genevieve, Littleheart and Jimmy Goodheart.
Joanna Nazario	To my loving family.
Joe Villafane	I dedicate this book to my family and my dog Tania.
Jonathan Rosner	I dedicate this book to my loving parents who challenge me everyday. I love them so.
Jordan Needle	I dedicate this book to the troops in Iraq.

Joseph Muraca	I dedicate this book to my family and Blizzard Entertainment.
Julia Rose Friedman	I dedicate this to my family and friends.
Julia Schifini	I dedicate this to the Guide Dog Foundation, who help people and dogs everyday.
Juliet Villani	I dedicate this to my family and friends.
Justine Martilloti	I dedicate this book to my family and friends for always being there for me.
Kaitlyn Emory	I dedicate this to my family and friends because I love them and they always stand by me.
Kara J. Dempsey	To my parents, my sister Ally, my cousins Jenna, Basil and Blue (my dogs) and my grandpa. I love you all! Thank you to Mrs. J. Cohen, Mrs. Klein and all the men and women in the service and the memory of Ann Frank and Princess Diana. Thanks for making me who I am (so far!).
Katie Smith	I dedicate this to my family, friends and anyone else who helped to work on this book.
Kaylee Condon	I dedicate this book to my family, friends and my two dogs, Riley and Cody.
Kelli Marie Cosentino	I dedicate this book to my mom. She has always been there for me and I think she deserves everything she earns because she is a very hard worker.
Kelly Morgese	I dedicate this book to my brother Brian, he joined the Navy on Sept. 8, 2004; he means the world to me and I miss him like crazy. Love you bro.
Kevin Archbold	I dedicate this to my mom for always encouraging me to read.
Kevin Harvey	I dedicate this to my mom Ellen, my dad Warren, and my younger sister Michele.
Kevin Metz	I dedicate this to my dog Heide 3/15/03 to 10/18/04.
Krystin White	I dedicate this book to my best friend Gabby and my family.

14

Kyle Vadnais	I dedicate this book to my family.
Laura Tejo	I dedicate this to my loving parents who will love me no matter what I do. I also dedicate it to my best friend Hannah Griesel.
Lauren Amatulli	I dedicate this book to my parents, brother and family. Also to all my friends.
Lauren Levin	I dedicate this book to all my family and friends, including my dog Woofy.
Lyla Stern	I dedicate this book to all of my friends who are always there, thank you guys so much!
Maria DiMatteo	I would like to thank my parents and all my English teachers at Old Mill Road School who always told me to write nonstop.
Maria Pokorny	I dedicate this book to my family and to my friends.
Marissa Zappala	I would like to dedicate this book to all my friends and teachers at Merrick Avenue Middle School and my family.
Matt Lagueras	I dedicate this to my best friends Gina, Martin, Michel and Kyle for being so nice to me since I was only four years old. I also dedicate this to all my family. Thank you for your time. Tell Gizmo I said hi.
Matt Neugeboren	I dedicate this to my family and friends, especially my parents.
Matthew Healy	To my mom, dad and two brothers.
Matthew Sperber	My dedication is to my family and friends.
Melissa Nuzzi	I dedicate this to my mom, dad and friends.
Metin Humet	I dedicate this book to my family.
Michael J. Iacono	I dedicate this book to my family.
Michael Mascaro	I dedicate this to my family and especially my English teacher, Mrs. Schwartz.
Michael Petassi	I dedicate this to my family and friends.
Molly Ratzker	I would like to dedicate this book to all those who believe in the beauty of their dreams and my family and friends who mean so much to me!

Moses Rodriguez	To my sick dog in the Dominican Republic, and to my entire family who is so important to me.
Nadia Marie Hernandez	I dedicate this book to Ms. Schwartz, the funniest English teacher.
Naomi Volk	To everyone and everything that have come into my life. Without you I wouldn't be who I am today.
Nicholas K. Taborsky	To all the soldiers who died and are still in Iraq, my friends and family.
Nick Landi	I dedicate this book to my friends and family and the soldiers who are fighting in Iraq.
Nicole Scialdone	I would like to dedicate this book to my animal loving family, Ms. Schwartz, Ms. Paltrowitz and "Gizmo" who helped teach us all about the importance of service dogs.
Paige Wolke	I would like to dedicate this book to my friends and family who have been so supportive of this project
Patricia Hazel	To all of the dogs that helped people out there and to my family and friends. Also to all of my teachers.
Patrick Goldberg	I dedicate this book to my Aunt Cathy.
Patrick Greene	I dedicate this book to my family, friends and relatives and the Tsunami survivors.
Rachel Israel	I dedicate this book to Murphy, my cousin's dog. Murphy died about two years ago from old age and we miss him dearly.
Rebecca Davidson	I dedicate this book to my loving parents and sister, who will always be there for me.
Robert Andrew McGetrick, Jr.	I dedicate this book to my dog, family and friends.
Ryan Charles	I dedicate this to my family and friends.
Samantha Costa	I dedicate this book to my family, friends and my dog, Princess!

16

Samantha Hollander	To my dog Astro who was always a hyper puppy and would have never changed, he will always be loved and missed!
Santino Larios	I dedicate this book to my family and friends.
Skye Friedman	To all my seventh grade friends and teachers.
Stacy Berkowitz	I dedicate this book to my family and my Portuguese water dog, Hudson.
Stephanie Frasca	To my friends, family and Mrs. Schwartz.
Stephanie Massucci	I would like to dedicate this book to all of my family and friends and everyone who has stood by me.
Stephanie Roney	To my loving family and my two dogs, Dixie and Sandy.
Stephen Giaco	I dedicate this to my family and friends.
Stuart Sacks	I would like to thank my Chatterton teachers without whom I would never be half the writer I am today.
Teddy Topper	I dedicate this book to my family, but especially to my Aunt Mary Anne, who I almost lost at 9-11.
Thalia Benavides	I would like to dedicate this to my family and friends. Also to my dog.
Timothy John Metzger	To my family and dog.
Thomas Burzynski	To everyone.
Thomas McKeon	I dedicate this book to my Nana who died from cancer. She loved to read.
Yael Bar-Giora	I dedicate this book to my whole family, especially to my dad Elan Bar-Giora.
Zachary Fox	I dedicate this book to my parents.
Zack Best	I dedicate this to all my loved ones.

Thank You, Mrs. Schwartz

"When we were little kids we would read stories with our parents and wonder how the author could accomplish something so amazing. Now, our wonder as a child returned when Mrs. Schwartz proudly announced that we would be writing our own book," wrote Hailey and Danielle, Mrs. Schwartz's students.

It's no surprise. For 30 years, Mrs. Ellen Schwartz has made language arts into an educational adventure. It was also no surprise when Mrs. Schwartz embraced the idea of writing a book with kids.

"The making of *Matthew's Tangled Trails*," Schwartz said about her first book with teens, "can be compared to gardening. Planting the seeds, cultivating the young minds of my students, and watching them grow tall with blossoms facing the sun, brings a teacher the greatest of pleasures."

Schwartz uses her easy connection with the kids and love of literature to make language arts a very real process. *Matthew's Tangled Trails* was a complex mystery, incorporating issues such as bullying, plagiarism, and group think into an exciting read. United States Senator from New York, Charles Schumer, commended her for the work.

Through team work and diligence, Mrs. Ellen Schwartz's seventh grade honor students along with writers Jeri Fink and Donna Paltrowitz have accomplished a tremendous feat. I commend all that participated in this project for their hard work..

Mrs. Schwartz met Gizmo in *Matthew's Tangled Trails*.

Mrs. Schwartz and some of the student- authors from *Corey's Web.*

Already a dog lover, she helped continue Gizmo's character in her next book, *Corey's Web Unleashed.* Her students spun a mystery involving a dog shelter, dognapping, and unabashed bullying. Naturally, Mrs. Schwartz's own dog, Max, made it into the story.

Mrs. Schwartz was ready to tackle nonfiction when she began planning for *The Gizmo Tales: Hero Dogs.* In this exciting, diverse book, Mrs. Schwartz takes her students -- and future readers -- through a canine world where character dominates. By the time they completed the book, the kids agreed on one thing: the world would be a better place if people

embraced the same qualities as hero dogs.

In *Matthew's Tangled Trails,* Mrs. Schwartz sent this message out to all student-authors, and the readers that have followed.

> Broaden your horizons
> And reach for the stars
> You won't need a ladder - -
> Just delve into the unknown
> With high expectations
> for you are our future.

Thank you, Mrs. Schwartz, for all you have given to your students and kids around the world!

What's a Gizmo?

Gizmo is a new critter called a labradoodle. Some people think he is a dog, but don't tell him that. He has big round eyes that look right into you, as if he is your best friend (even if you've only known him a few minutes). He can read words in three different languages, obey hand signals, and snatch a flying peanut-butter-and-jelly sandwich in a flash. When it comes to food, he can best be described as a living vacuum cleaner. With this same enthusiasm for food, Gizmo seeks out the companionship of people, especially kids.

Gizmo was born in Australia, on a farm called Rutland Manor. He comes from a healthy line of labradoodles -- dogs bred to help people. Way back in his family there was a labrador retriever and a poodle, hence Gizmo's breed. Some people say that Gizmo falls in the category of "designer mutt," which is a goofy name for a sweet, loving pup. Gizmo doesn't mind when you call him that. Between his monthly haircuts, and his ability not to trigger allergy attacks in two-legged critters, he is paws above most canines.

Gizmo is a therapy dog, trained to help people feel better about their problems. He wears a tag, and carries an ID card from *Therapy Dogs International*. Because of his credentials, Gizmo's part-time work is to visit places where you would not ordinarily expect to see a dog -- such as libraries, schools, and community centers. Gizmo's full-time job is to make reading and writing a fun, but an important part of life. He visits classes and works with students to write, edit, and illustrate their own books. When the collaborative books are finished, Book Web publishes and distributes them around the world. Gizmo's curly-haired face is always on the cover.

Gizmo's books are about dogs, people, and all the powerful work that we can accomplish together. Because Gizmo's books are written by kids, the stories reveal our world from their perspective. This book is about real heroes -- both four and two-legged types -- that make a difference in our world. Meet the dogs who have rescued people, as well as, the people who have rescued dogs. Although many great canines in history are not included in our text books, they have played important roles in our world. Glimpse some presidential pups that show us a very different

20

side to the people who are in the history books.

Gizmo and his heroes show us how much we can accomplish by embracing the right qualities in our lives. It didn't take 133 students long to realize that Gizmo's friendliness is contagious. He extends a paw for everyone to play, hug, talk, and be included. He reaches out to connect people with the qualities that really make a difference in our lives. Gizmo brings along an awareness of loyalty, courage, friendship, respect, and love, creating that special bond to empower people to make the world a better place. For this, Gizmo is our hero.

Gizmo taking his little sister Coco out for a joy ride.

Table of Contents

From Jeri and Donna

Heroes teach us about the good things in life. They tell us anything is possible if we strive for the best in human spirit.

This book is about canine heroes -- dogs that teach us about loyalty, devotion, courage, and love. Canine heroes don't ask questions or look for sound bytes on the evening news -- they just act. Their stories speak far louder than words. The dogs in this book are role models for our own behavior, instinctively demonstrating qualities that are often hard to find in today's world.

When you read these stories, think about the hero dogs and what they did in a single act or an ongoing commitment to human service. They made a difference, sending messages of hope to the people in their lives. Perhaps the ability for dogs to teach us is best said in this story written by David, a young soldier in the Middle East, in an area scarred by terrorism.

There are wild dogs that roam around the surrounding towns.
One day, we saw the most amazing sight. One of our tool
sheds started making strange noises. Upon further inspection,
we found that one of the female dogs had given birth to six
puppies. It was the cutest thing in the world. These little
creatures were all bundled up together while the mom watched
over them. Later on, it started to rain. Not just a light rain, but
bordering on hail. The puppies were getting attacked by these
little pieces of ice. The poor creatures were wet and cold.
I didn't know what to do. They were freezing to death. Never
mind the terrorists, and never mind the dangerous towns,
these were puppies and someone had to take action! Then
something incredible happened. The mother dog came out of
nowhere and saved the day. One by one, she picked up each
puppy in her mouth, and delivered them to safety underneath
one of the rocks. I tried to help, but when I picked up one
of the puppies, the mother looked at me as if to say,
"Thanks, but no thanks. I got this."

It was such a sight. In this town, amidst all of the fear and
violence, here is a mother dog caring for her young. It was
unbelievable. Suddenly I realized what a dangerous place
I was in, and how I could really worry the people who cared
about me most. I called my mom that day to say, "I love you."

The heroic stories in this book bring hope into our lives. Like the soldier, they teach us the value of life filled with courage and love. Over and over again, you will hear the student-authors describe these dogs as loyal, dedicated, trustworthy, brave, and loving. These are the qualities that make a difference in all of our lives. They enable people to make our world a better place -- from classrooms and neighborhoods, to cities, states, and countries. Perhaps these dogs can teach us something very important about the human joy of life.

Everyday Heroes

There are approximately 60 million pet dogs just in the United States. In fact, a majority of homes have at least one pet dog or cat. These pets are more than animals living in human homes -- they are members of the family, sharing daily lives with their people. Their numbers are constantly growing -- and that doesn't even include the six to eight million *potential* pets that enter shelters each year!

There are purebreds, mixed breeds, and "designer mutts" that are family pets. Some are big, some are small, some are shy, and some can't wait to greet the next person through the front door. Sometimes, one of these pets is called upon to act beyond their daily roles. Maybe it's a house fire or a medical emergency. Perhaps it's a threatening stranger or a physical attack. Whatever the reason, instinct takes over, transforming a sweet pet into a fierce protector with one goal -- *keep my human safe*.

Here are a few stories of these everyday heroes. There are many other stories that never made it to the newspapers or television. Dogs don't care about publicity -- they only want to make sure their humans are with them.

Consider this -- the next time your pet dog wants to play or cuddle, remember that he or she might be the next everyday hero!

Arthur, from the Rossi family

Bentley, from the Grosswirth family

**Michael and Minx
from the Schiff family**

**Dana and Mickey from
the Berkowtiz family**

Coco, Gizmo's little sister

AUTUMN written by:

Jordan

Daniel

Alexander

Michael

When Debbie Marvit-McGlothlin and her husband John rescued a dog from a shelter, they had no idea how the dog would dramatically return the favor.

On September 14, they went to a rescue shelter for abandoned animals. The shelter was located on a farm not far from their house on the north side of Pittsburgh, Pennsylvania. There were 30 squirming, excited puppies when they arrived. Debbie and John had a tough decision. Which dog should they choose? Little did they know that they were making a life-or-death decision.

After much thought, they couldn't take their eyes off the sweet shepherd/hound mix with her funny "super long ears." The couple selected her, and then chose the name Autumn because of the puppy's fall-like colors and the time of year. Autumn went home to live with Debbie, John, and their two other dogs, Jackson, a brindle pitbull/boxer mix and Penny, a brindle/terrier mix. Autumn took up a special place in Debbie's heart. Debbie described the puppy as "my little sweetie."

Autumn as a puppy

Time passed and Debbie found out she was pregnant. Everyone was really excited about the newcomer into the family. Around the same time, Autumn started acting strangely. She sniffed continuously around a mole on the back of Debbie's thigh.

At first, Autumn just sniffed the mole. Then she began to lick it for hours and hours. She would also paw at it. The mole was on the back of my thigh so if it wasn't for Autumn, I never would have noticed it.

Debbie wasn't concerned about Autumn's bizarre behavior. Debbie had no pain or discomfort in that area of her leg. In contrast, she felt strong and healthy, energized by her pregnancy, and looking forward to becoming a mother. Autumn wouldn't give up. The dog became more aggressive, pawing, licking, and sniffing at the mole. "I'd walk down the stairs and she'd be biting or scratching at my leg," Debbie recollected.

Debbie and Autumn

Four months passed, and Autumn continued relentlessly pawing at the mole. Finally, Debbie could no longer ignore her beloved dog. During a trip to the doctor, Debbie asked to have the mole checked out. She told the doctor the story about Autumn's strange behavior. Both the doctor and Debbie felt that there was nothing wrong. However, the doctor decided to be safe and do a biopsy.

No one would have predicted the results. The mole was a malignant melanoma -- the most serious form of skin cancer. Melanoma kills 8000 people a year just in the United States. As with all cancers, early detection is the key to recovery. The doctors quickly removed Debbie's melanoma, along with surrounding skin tissue. Fortunately, the cancer had not spread to other parts of her body. Debbie is clear about what happened.

I believe that Autumn saved my life.

Debbie wore a bandage for three weeks after the melanoma was removed. Autumn never went near the spot again.

The only other time that Autumn behaved in a similar manner was with a dog owned by Debbie's parents. Autumn always licked the dog's lips. The veterinarian had diagnosed a tumor, but the dog was too old and frail to undergo surgery.

Can Autumn really detect cancer? Other people have reported that their dogs sniffed out different diseases or medical conditions. Some working dogs are trained to alert people to health problems such as seizures, sleep disorders, high blood pressure, low blood sugar, and migraines.

Dogs can track a lot of things, from missing people and drugs, to hidden cookies. Although humans have about 5 million olfactory receptors, dogs' noses have more than 200 million. It's no surprise that human noses can't compete with their canine counterparts.

Dr. Kirkwood, Director of the Melanoma and Skin Cancer Program Center at the University of Pittsburgh Cancer Institute, theorizes that it is a result of their carnivorous background. He believes the dogs smell the blood from cracks in the skin around the melanoma. However, Kirkwood suggests it is probably more complicated. Dogs like Autumn may demonstrate an ability to recognize molecular markers of certain cancers, and respond by alerting the stricken person.

A study published in the British Medical Journal found some compelling results. Six dogs were trained to identify people with bladder cancer on the basis of urine odor. When the dogs were presented with a collection of urine samples from both healthy and sick people, they were able to detect the cancer victims 41 percent of the time. The researchers made it as difficult as possible, but they could not stop the dogs. Scientists are hopeful that one day dogs can be trained to reliably detect certain forms of cancer by smell, helping doctors to diagnose and treat these diseases far earlier than our present technology allows.

Debbie and John's baby was born four months after her melanoma was removed. The baby was named John Wesley McGlothlin III. The cancer had no effect on Debbie's pregnancy or the baby. Now baby John plays with the gentle, intuitive Autumn. When John cries, Autumn gives him a loving "kiss." In their neighborhood, everyone knows how lucky the McGlothlin family is to have Autumn. She is a true, everyday hero.

Autumn in the snow

30

NOSEY DOGS

Dogs relate to the world primarily through the sense of smell. They can smell odors we don't even know exist.

Illustration by Jennifer Kotler

While scenthounds such as bloodhounds, bassett hounds, and beagles are well known for their olfactory abilities, many different pure and mixed breed dogs use their noses to help people do things such as:

*track criminals
*find missing people
*hunt wild animals
*locate drugs
*detect explosives and terrorists
*uncover contraband
*expose smuggled (illegal) materials
*detect medical conditions such as epilepsy, low
   blood sugar, migraines and heart attacks
*find people buried in the snow
*locate drowning victims
*find corpses in natural disasters
*locate bodies in building collapses
*detect different forms of cancer, including skin,
   breast, and prostate

31

LARI *written by:*

| Julia | Amanda | Billy | Paige | Jennifer |

Lari is a friendly Labrador retriever ready to greet anyone who enters the Bristel home. This time something was different.

Diane, Debbie and Bill's teenage daughter, was home alone, speaking on the telephone with her mother. The doorbell rang and something scared Diane. Lari sensed it immediately. The dog peered around the teenager and saw a frightening-looking man. He said he was there to ask about the vacant lot next door. Diane told the stranger that her father would be home soon, but the man refused to leave.

Debbie, on the other end of the telephone, could do nothing. The storm door to the house was closed, but not locked. Suddenly, the man tried to shove his way into the house. Gentle Lari knew it was time to take action. She squeezed herself between Diane and the stranger, forcing the man back out the door.

Lari in the snow

Unwilling to confront the large, protective dog, the man fled. Later, the police tracked him down and discovered he had a long criminal record. Debbie knew exactly what happened.

Dogs take their cue from our voice, body posture, and language. When we speak quickly in a high pitch, and are tense, they know something is not right.

It wasn't until that frightening afternoon that the Bristel family realized how lucky they were to have Lari. No one knows what could have happened if the man had successfully forced his way into the house. The Bristels had always protected Lari; this time, Lari kept Diane safe. Although Lari is an everyday hero, she has a very important job. She is a breeder dog for the Guide Dog Foundation.

Portrait of Lari
by Julia Schifini

Lari, a black Labrador retriever, was different right from the beginning. Labradors make great guide dogs for a variety of reasons. The dogs are the right size to guide a person, but not so big that they would be unable to use public transportation. They are very smart, physically strong, don't have to be groomed often, and love all kinds of weather. Labrador retrievers are well known for their eagerness to please their human family. Recently, the Guide Dog Foundation started breeding labradoodles -- a mix between a standard poodle and a Labrador retriever. They started breeding them because some people are allergic to dog fur. Labradoodles have hair that makes them hypoallergenic. They look just like Gizmo!

Lari was born into the last litter of puppies for her mom. The breeder mom was being retired. Two puppies were chosen to be future breeders, Lari and one of her sisters. Although her future would be different than her siblings, Lari had to be raised and trained like the others.

Sponsored by The Lion's Club, Lari moved into the Bristel home for her puppy year. She went through the same basic obedience and socialization as the other puppies. She was trained as a guide dog and required to pass the rigid test given by the Foundation. However, when the training was completed, Lari went back to the Bristel's home.

The Bristels are puppy walkers with the Guide Dog Foundation. Puppy walkers provide loving homes for puppies until they are old enough to be trained as guide dogs for blind and visually impaired people. Puppy walkers housebreak the puppy, socialize it in many different environments, and provide much-needed attention. Puppies move in with their families at about seven to eight weeks old and remain for a year. They return to the Guide Dog Foundation for training and pairing with a disabled person. The Guide Dog Foundation gives these highly trained dogs, completely free of charge, to people who need them.

Like Lari, the Bristel family is also an everyday hero. They have been

Lari's puppies

puppy walkers for nine years, housing 16 different dogs from the Guide Dog Foundation. Some stayed with the Bristels for the entire year, others had different experiences. Debbie explains:

Some of our pups are waiting for their puppy walker families to come from other states. Some have been retiring mommies, dogs waiting for a new family. It has been great fun. Puppies give unconditional love to their humans. Seeing our puppies graduate and go off to work helping visually impaired people live independent lives, is a wonderful experience.

Lari stays with the Bristels until she's ready to have her pups. At that point, she's moved to the nursery at the Guide Dog Foundation.

Lari has had several litters of beautiful, healthy, very smart puppies. In December, three-quarters of all the puppies in the nursery at the Foundation were related to Lari. Most were her grandchildren. Soon she'll retire and be a great-grandmother.

In the Bristel home, Lari has a lot of company. There's Debbie, her husband Bill, and their 17-year old Diane. There is also April Sunshine XII, a golden retriever, Cadbury the rabbit, fish, and neighborhood cats that come to visit. It's a wonderful environment for a breeder guide dog like Lari.

These days, Lari is back to her playful ways -- munching carrots and stealing bagels whenever she can get away with it. The Bristels know how fortunate they are to have such an incredible dog in their family.

A true hero is driven by the courage to fight and protect loved ones. Although Lari was already doing a heroic job as a breeder dog, no one would have guessed that she would defiantly put herself in direct danger to protect her beloved family.

Puppy Pin-Ups

Meet Maria Nuzzi -- one of the women at the Guide Dog Foundation who helps puppy walkers with their precious charges. She's holding Freddy, a nine-week old puppy on his way from the nursery to his puppy walker family. Here are some puppy pin-ups of these amazing dogs.

LISSY *written by:*

Laura   **Anthony**   **Christina**   **Lyla**

Dogs get lost all the time. Imagine a dog that was lost and found across the Atlantic Ocean, in another country. Meet Lissy, a champion German shepherd.

One day a resident in the Town of Babylon on Long Island, New York, spotted a stray German shepherd wandering through the streets. The resident quickly reported it to the local animal shelter. Animal

Control Officer Kristin Siarkowicz was notified. She searched the streets for the homeless dog. By the time she found the dog, the shelter had closed, so Siarkowicz brought the ragged animal to the veterinary hospital. Siarkowicz knew immediately that the German shepherd was not an ordinary stray.

I recognized her as being special. I could tell just by looking at her, that she had very good body structure and temperament . . . the look of a dog bred to the German conformation standard.

Canine conformation describes the general quality of a dog's physical structure, when standing still and moving. The term refers to how much an individual dog conforms to the ideal standard for that breed. There are conformation standards for each breed. Conformation shows and competitions are held all over the world.

Conformation standards for German shepherds vary among the

leading organizations. They include features such as strength, agility, alertness, a direct and fearless temperament without hostility, smooth, rhythmic gait, black nose, deep but not too-broad chest, and a lively, intelligent look in the eyes. German conformation standards for the breed are some of the most demanding in the world.

Portrait of Lissy
by Christina Strezenec

When Lissy finally arrived at the shelter, she was quiet and reserved, probably in what Siarkowicz refers to as a "state of shock." The Animal Control Officer speculated that a dog of Lissy's breeding did not know what to do when she was put into a cage in a strange environment, surrounded by barking dogs. Eventually, Siarkowicz noticed that the dog had a tattoo. Canine tattoos are not very common. More often, a dog will have a tiny microchip inserted at the back of the neck, that can be scanned for identification. Using the tattoo number, B-C6632, Siarkowicz contacted someone who could look in the registry of all German shepherds that have ever received a tattoo. Armed with that information, the next step was to find her registered name. Everyone was amazed at the stray dog's full name:

V Lissy von der Posthalterey Ahlen SchH III

"Lissy" was her "call name." When a litter is registered in Germany, the puppies must have names that start with the same first letter. With each new litter, the breeder moves on to the next letter in the alphabet. *Poshalterey Ahlen* is the kennel name. *Posthalterey* is an old way of saying "post office" and *Ahlen* is a town in southwest Germany. *SchH III* is the abbreviation for Schutzhund III, a German sport that encompasses three phases of training: tracking, obedience, and protection. A dog can reach levels I to III in this demanding sport. Lissy ranked at the highest level, a III. The *V* in Lissy's name refers to her conformation rating -- the highest possible rank. Lissy was a real winner!

How did a champion Schutzhund end up so far from home in an

Officer Siarkowicz and her dogs, Abel (left), Heddy Sue, Peppercorn

animal shelter? Lissy was shown in Germany and rated at *V6* because she placed 6th in her class of nearly 100 competing dogs. She was bred three times in Germany and sold for $10,000 to a man in Brooklyn, New York. He purchased Lissy to breed with another male Schutzhund III. Under his care, Lissy was attacked by another dog who severely damaged her ear. The Brooklyn man shipped Lissy to a breeder on Long Island, New York. Suddenly, Lissy was gone! The man on Long Island never said anything, so there was no followup. Eventually Lissy was picked up as a stray.

When Lissy's story went public, German shepherd lovers all over the United States and Europe advocated for her safety. Joanne Anderson wrote in an article in the *Beacon*:

> *"Don't let anything happen to Lissy!" was the message over and over again. People offered to help Herding Dog Rescue. A dog training school in Texas wanted to adopt her so she could be an obedience star there for the rest of her life. Officer Siarkowicz preferred to keep her nearby.*

Siarkowicz had a lot of ideas. She brought Lissy out to a field and discovered that the dog performed like she had never missed a day of training. Siarkowicz was astounded. Lissy hadn't done anything for several years, yet she hadn't forgotten anything. It was clear that Lissy, after all her troubles, deserved a very special family. Siarkowicz choose the Manzi family. Joe Manzi owns a food/training facility for dogs called, *Total Pet Care* in Holbook, New York. His wife, Dawn, and two children are ardent dog lovers! Manzi tells what happened next.

> *We officially adopted Lissy in May, when she was eight years old. We were renting a house at the time and we weren't supposed to have a large dog, so Officer Siarkowicz helped us by keeping Lissy with her. She would come back and forth for visits until we moved into our own house, and could stay full time. Lissy LOVES Officer Siarkowicz. It's really great to see them together.*

Lissy now lives with the Manzi family in their Hampton, Long Island home. There's Dawn, her husband Joe, 12-year old Jade, and two-year old Joseph. Joanne Anderson wrote a follow-up in the *Beacon*.

Lissy has plenty to do in her new home these days. She thinks she's a European au pair. If her two-year old toddler friend is in the yard and goes anywhere near the water, Lissy blocks his path with her frame. "Oh, no, you're not, kinder" she says with German shepherd body language. Lissy, enjoy the lovely life you have earned.

The Manzi family gives Lissy the love and attention she deserves. In return, Lissy makes her new family feel safe and protected. Lissy has her own bed and toy basket. She even went to school as Joseph's "show-and-tell." Dawn realizes that Lissy's quality of life must include activity and thought. She makes time to do things with Lissy, and in turn finds time for herself. "Lissy has made a real difference in my life," Dawn says.

Lissy may not have saved a life or caught a criminal. Instead, she showed the world about the power of courage, determination, and perseverance. She proved that anything is possible, and how important it is never to give up hope. Not many people could have survived Lissy's experiences and remained strong and loving. Lissy makes it clear to all of us that no matter what you go through, you have to stay strong and not let it get you down. That is the stuff of a real everyday hero!

> *My name is Jade Manzi and I am 12 years old. Lissy is my dog. Having her in our family has been great! She's energetic, full of life, and always makes me feel safe and secure. Everything about Lissy is special. If I had to choose one talent that really stands above the rest, I would say that Lissy's ability to sense people's feelings is pretty amazing. Most of all, Lissy makes me feel happy because I know that I always have someone to play with.*

ODIN written by:

Juliet   Briana   Aly   Naomi   Deanna

Odin had been nervous all night.

The Labrador/pit bull mix wouldn't stop pacing in front of a specific wall. Figuring that the dog would eventually calm down, Theresa took Holly, the toy poodle, and went to bed. Theresa Michelsen and her husband Russ, had adopted Odin from a local shelter. Theresa recalls what Odin looked like as a puppy.

He was so small, he could fit in the palm of my hand.

Odin was jet black with a white spot on his chest and back paw --

the runt in his tiny litter of three puppies. The Labrador/pit bull mix quickly grew into what he is today -- a big, gentle, 80 pound dog. Theresa describes him:

Odin is very smart, and can be pretty protective at home and in his yard. He is also very affectionate, vocal, and aware of his surroundings.

Portrait of Odin
by Naomi Volk

When Holly, the toy poodle, joined the family, she was twice as big as Odin was at the same age. Holly never grew like her brother. Eventually, she reached a total of seven pounds, less than one-tenth Odin's size. Because he's so gentle, Odin allows the bossy poodle to

40

Odin

rule. He doesn't care that he's older and has over 70 pounds on the tiny dog.

On October 31, Halloween night, the Michelsen family was busy. Russ, the father, loves to fish. He had taken the time to visit his parents in Montauk Point, at the eastern end of Long Island, New York. Montauk sits on the Atlantic Ocean and offers some of the best fishing in the area. It's a long ride from the family's home in Levittown. Theresa and Russ's kids, Jillian and Ryan, went to a Halloween/birthday party for Ryan's girlfriend, Nicole.

Throughout the night, Odin continued to pace. He seemed to stay near that same wall, pawing, sniffing, and walking back and forth.

At two in the morning, Jillian, Ryan, Nicole, and Nicole's mom returned to the house. Ryan went to sleep in his bedroom upstairs, right next to Theresa's room. The girls didn't go to sleep right away. It was perhaps the best choice they had ever made in their lives. Instead, they stayed up, sitting in the kitchen with Karen, Nicole's mom, talking and having a good time.

Portrait of Odin
by Deanna Werthauer

Suddenly, at 4 A.M., Jillian, Karen, and Nicole heard a strange clicking sound. Odin started to race, barking wildly. They told the dog to quiet down, but Odin refused to listen. The dog became frantic. He ran to the foot of the stairs, looked up, and barked as loud as he could. Finally, the girls decided to see why Odin was fussing so much. They followed him through the living room and to the stairs.

That's when they smelled the smoke.

They raced upstairs to get Theresa, Ryan, and Holly before it was too late. Theresa shuddered, remembering what happened.

Ryan's room was completely engulfed in flames. My room was filled with smoke.

Everyone rushed out of the burning house.

Later, the firemen concluded it was an electrical fire that started in the fuse box -- right where Odin had paced back and forth, early in the evening. The dog sensed something in the walls long before the fire took hold and spread. Eventually, the fire crept through the walls to the upstairs. It burst into Ryan's room. Ryan would have lasted about three more minutes if the girls hadn't woken him. The fire was just moving into Theresa's room. She had a little more time than Ryan, but without help, Theresa and Holly would have died also.

Ryan spent a few days in the hospital, recovering from smoke inhalation and carbon monoxide poisoning. The house was seriously damaged -- it took more than one year to repair.

Odin saved all of them. Perhaps his name had something to do with it. When Odin was a puppy, the Michelsen family wanted to name him Hershey or Oreo. No one was happy with the name, so Russ stepped in and chose Odin. Odin is the name of the most powerful Viking god in Norse mythology. No one could have predicted how Odin would grow into his name.

Odin received a medal and special recognition in the local Blessing of the Animals. Odin saved the lives of five people and one bossy toy poodle -- an amazing act of courage and heroism.

Briana Cangemi's interpretation of Odin's Story

Odin's Family Scrapbook

Odin's awards

Odin with his medal

Russ, Odin, and Theresa

SMOKEY JOE *written by:*

Marissa

Heather

Maria

Ben

Winnett, Montana — Not only is Smokey Joe a hero and all around working dog, he's a beloved companion, goes everywhere with me, and sleeps on my bed at night. He loves people and is gentle and loving with my grandkids.
I think it's great that you're undertaking the difficult task of writing and publishing a book. My cowboy hat's off to you!

Susan Stone (Buckaroo Sue) and Smokey Joe

When Smokey Joe disobeyed Susan's orders, it saved her life.

Smokey Joe had been told to stay out of the corral "because a dog makes cows very nervous when they are calving. The heifers (young cows) see the dog as a danger to their babies." Smokey Joe, as usual, circled all the way around the corral so he could "keep an eye" on Susan. The dog always obeyed her commands. Susan pushed open the gate and suddenly, in a "blink of an eye" the heifer attacked.

The two-year old Black Angus heifer had stalled in calving. Simply put, her baby calf was just too big to birth. Cattle rancher Susan Stone and her co-workers put straps on the soon-to-be born calf's feet. It was standard practice to help a heifer having difficulty giving birth. Ranchers try to be gentle, but it's really painful for the cow. Susan explains:

Usually cows and heifers DO NOT attack a person, but on a rare occasion right after giving birth and for another two days, these new bovine mothers can be very protective of their babies.

The day was one of those rare occasions. The heifer ran Susan and her boss right out of the pen. No one wanted to be near the angry mom.

The next day seemed different. Susan returned with Smokey Joe. The heifer had quieted down, and Susan decided that she was safe. There was another newborn calf that needed to be put in the barn, but the ornery heifer was in the way. Susan figured there was no problem.

She told Smokey Joe to "stay out" and went to work. The 45-pound dog stayed outside. Smokey Joe is a mix of three kinds of breeding dogs: Queensland blue heeler, Australian shepherd, and border collie. "Smokey Joe is so friendly," says Susan. "I can see all three breeds in him by how he acts, looks, and works livestock."

Susan first met Smokey Joe during breakfast at the world famous Jersey Lilly, a historic old western saloon and eatery. At the time, Susan had been working for the Lazy Diamond Six Ranch in Sand Springs, Montana. Susan lives nearby, in Winnett, Montana. Winnett is in a county called Petroleum-- the third least populated county in the United States.

The country around here is open rolling prairie and sage brush range, with interesting buttes and coulees. As you go north toward the Missouri River the land becomes very rugged and has pine covered ridges. We have four distinct seasons here, a very

Smokey Joe

cold and often snowy winter, a wonderful spring when everything is being born and blooming, a hot, dry summer, and a beautiful fall, often with an Indian summer.

She was having a leisurely breakfast at Jersey Lilly when a local woman appeared, trying to give away some puppies. She had two cute pups to offer. Susan refused because she already had an older dog. She was just about finished with breakfast when the woman returned with a different puppy in her arms. "Was he ever cute," Susan said, "and he immediately tried to get in my arms and lick my face. I was hooked and Smokey Joe had a new home."

Smokey Joe learned quickly. On his first day with Susan, he followed her everywhere and learned to "sit" on command. He even tried to work the heifers. It took several days before Susan chose his name.

A long time ago I had been in love with someone who had called me a Smokey Eyed witch, so I thought of the pup and he seemed to like the name Smokey Joe, so it stuck.

After a few months, Smokey Joe started to work on the ranch. He has many jobs, like herding the cows to eat, rounding up and getting the cows into the corral, keeping livestock on the trail and in the right direction, and helping Susan get the cows into the chute near the pen. Susan describes her work.

Being a cattle rancher is truly my calling in life and Smokey Joe makes my job much easier. Because he's so obedient, I can tell him to "get back" when I don't need his help and direct him to do my bidding when I do need his assistance. He's always watching out for me.

Smokey Joe weighs 45 pounds; heifers weigh 1000 pounds. Full grown cows weigh 1400 pounds, and a bull can hit a ton! He's an amazing "little" dog!

Nothing was more amazing than the day Susan re-entered the pen of

46

the "ornery heifer." Susan tells the story:

> *The heifer came out of the shed like a runaway freight train, blowing
> snot and bellering. She had me knocked down before I could
> formulate a plan for retreat . . . she had murder in her eye.
> I knew she was inflicting some pretty serious injuries. Suddenly
> something that looked and sounded like a cross between a buzz
> saw and porcupine streaked into the pen toward that heifer
> with a ferocity that would have scared Lucifer himself!*

Smokey Joe had chosen not to listen to Susan's command. He made one of those rare independent cowdog decisions that, "rules be damned, the lady was in dire need of his canine capabilities." Smokey Joe confronted the "heifer-from-hell." The fight to save Susan's life was on! The dog attacked the raging heifer that was over 20 times his size.

Smokey Joe saved Susan's life. The heifer "quit me in a heart-beat and took on her new adversary." Suddenly, Smokey Joe was under attack. The 1000-pound heifer was no match for the dog. Susan staggered out of the corral. Smokey Joe followed, once the heifer retreated. Susan wasn't safe yet. She stumbled her way back to the house and dialed 911. The EMTs showed up and rushed her to the hospital. Susan had suffered fractured ribs and vertebrae, a punctured lung, several bruised organs, a ruptured spleen, and serious internal bleeding.

Smokey Joe was a real hero. The first thing he won was a steak dinner from the boss. PetCo then gave him a gift certificate.

His most prestigious honor was the Dog Hero of the Year Award, sponsored by Kibbles 'n Bits and Del Monte Foods. Since 1954, the award has been given to a dog that best represents ". . . the bravery, intelligence, and loyalty of man's best friend."

As soon as it was possible, Susan and Smokey Joe went back to work. Susan still claims that Smokey Joe is the best ranch dog she has ever had. "Without him, I wouldn't be here."

To this day, Smokey Joe doesn't let a cow within ten feet of his beloved Susan.

Kibbles 'n Bits

Certificate of Merit

In recognition of your pet's courageous act, faithful companionship and caring heart. Kibbles 'n Bits would like to honor your dog in the

49th Annual Dog Hero of the Year Contest

Todd R. Lachman
Managing Director, Pet Products
Del Monte Foods

DOG HERO
of the year

Smokey Joe is working the sheep in this photo. All I have to do is open the gate and he brings in a small bunch of them.

Smokey Joe is standing in the shadow of me and my horse. Can you see him? We had to move 200 head of cows over sixty miles.

Smokey Joe works the cattle through the squeeze chute.

This photo was taken shortly after I was injured. I followed along in the pickup. Smokey Joe is bringing the bulls to the corrals by himself.

Dog Hero Of The Year

SUNDANCE written by:

| Heather | Brian | Stuart | Francesca |

Intruders and pythons are not supposed to show up in your backyard. It took a dog named Sundance to keep the property safe for one family.

Sundance, a playful golden retriever, was special from the beginning. He was a tiny, chunky puppy. Michelle Passalacqua recalls that, "I fell in love with the little gold butterball right away." Michelle took him home to live with her family, which today includes her husband, Anthony, daughters Kaila and Sara, and a large assembly of pets: a German shepherd, three cats, and ten parrots.

Gentle, loyal Sundance fit in well, quickly taking on the role as family (and pet) protector. When Sara was a baby, Sundance would put his front paws up on the baby gate and lower his head so she could hug him. "He has also raised kittens and a raccoon, taking care of everyone," Michelle adds.

When Sundance was only seven months old, he and Michelle were home with then 18-month old Kaila. It was late at night and Michelle let Sundance out to eat on their closed-in porch. Michelle had a strange feeling that someone was watching her. She turned quickly and saw a dangerous-looking man lurking outside her kitchen window. She shrieked and grabbed the telephone to dial 911. Sundance wasn't about to wait for a phone call. He heard Michelle's screams and took off, chasing the man. The man screamed and ran away. Michelle remembers the incident very clearly.

The police came and said I was very lucky to have such a brave puppy.

What does a brave puppy have to do with backyards and pythons?

Sundance's most heroic act occurred on a warm, sunny day in August. Seven-year old Kaila and three-year old Sara decided to have a picnic in their backyard. Michelle and Kaila left for a few minutes to go into the house for drinks. Sara and Sundance were alone. Michelle wasn't concerned; she was confident that Sundance would watch over Kaila. The little girl sat down happily to play in her new toy ball pit. Suddenly Michelle and Kaila heard screams. Michelle rushed to her child.

Sara was on top of the picnic table crying hysterically. Sundance was barking at a huge, eight-foot long *dead* snake.

It was horribly clear what had happened. The python had made the toy ball pit its home. When Sara went to play, the snake slithered towards her. A hungry python can be lethal to a small child. Sundance jumped in front of the snake to protect Sara -- then attacked. The golden retriever bit the python in the back of its head and killed it.

Sara was safe. Sundance was safe. Neither one had been bitten by the snake. Sundance had recognized that Sara was in danger and leaped in to protect her, never considering the danger to himself. No one ever found out where the snake came from, or how the African python found the toy ball bit in the Passalacqua's backyard.

Sundance is a courageous dog. He thought only of Sara, and not what could happen to him. He was loyal, brave, and determined to protect his family. Most of all, he was willing to lay down his life for Sara. This made him an extraordinary hero, worthy of becoming the Kibbles 'n Bits Dog Hero of the Year.

Working Dog Heroes

"Feed the fish," the announcement was heard on the luxury cruise ship. "If you don't get rid of it, the dogs will be sitting at your suitcases."

"The dogs" are canine detection teams trained to sniff out contraband smuggled illegally into the country. Whether it's insect-infected fruit left innocently in a jacket pocket, or a stash of illegal drugs, the dogs will find it. The reality is simple -- it's tough to fool a working dog!

Working dogs are a breed unto themselves. They hold jobs almost as varied as human professions, from service occupations to the military. We see them everywhere, but often don't know exactly what they *do*. Most of us have observed a guide dog helping a blind or visually impaired person. Many of us don't even know that there are dogs trained to help deaf or hearing impaired people. Known as service dogs, these canines assist people who suffer from a wide range of disabilities, doing tasks that would seem impossible without hands or speech! Working dogs are also found in police departments, fire departments, and the military. There are even canines trained to detect terrorists!

Working dogs all have one thing in common -- they're trained to serve the needs of their humans. While they don't receive the same recognition as people, these hero dogs are on the job daily, demonstrating the selfless dedication that inspires all who know them.

Firedogs Memorial
Bide-A-Wee Memorial Park

Zoie, a seizure dog, takes a rest.

Mrs. Schwartz and Gizmo, a therapy dog

Bruno, a guide dog

Murphy, a hospital therapy dog

BOOMER *written by:*

Alex   Lauren   Michael   Matt   Corey

It was three in the morning when Suffolk County Police Officer John Mallia and his dog Boomer, were called. A man had beaten up his girlfriend and fled from their home, leaving her bruised and bloodied.

Boomer went to work putting his nose to the ground, tracking the attacker, hidden in dense bushes about one block away. The man could see the ominous-looking German shepherd nearing his hideout. Choosing to take the offensive, the man leaped from the bushes and lunged at the dog, a lethal, six-inch knife in his hand.

Boomer ignored the danger and went right for the attacker. The man plunged the knife, over and over again into the dog. Boomer was stabbed a total of six times. One of the wounds just missed his eye. Boomer did not give up. He had a job to do, and the astounding dog would not let anything, or anyone, stop him. Boomer doesn't know *how* to give up.

Mallia moved in behind his canine partner and the attacker slashed the officer's hand with the knife. Boomer still wouldn't let go. It had turned into a life-and-death struggle for the indomitable German shepherd.

Finally, the backup police arrived. They moved in on the man, and Boomer and Officer Mallia backed off. It was a tough collar, but the police prevailed. The man was arrested and brought straight to jail. Officer Mallia went to the hospital and had stitches put in his hand.

Boomer was rushed to Coram Animal Hospital for emergency surgery. For three hours, Boomer's life was hanging by a thread. No one was sure the incredibly brave dog would survive his stab wounds.

The perpetrator was charged with second-degree assault, injuring a police animal, aggravated cruelty to an animal, resisting arrest, and harassment. Officer Mallia was treated and released from the hospital later that morning.

"Boomer is expected to make a full recovery," the attending veterinarian finally reported at the end of the surgery. For Boomer, it was an understatement. The loyal police dog, and 9-11 canine veteran, would not let stab wounds and surgery keep him down. In less than a month, Boomer was back on the job with his partner.

Heroes come in all different shapes and sizes. You may find a living hero like a fireman or a soldier. There are mythical heroes like Achilles and Ajax. Not many of us think about heroes like Boomer, who spends his life helping and protecting the public. If everyone had Boomer's courage, determination, and spirit, this would be a much better world for all of us.

Boomer is a German shepherd, perfect for police work. German shepherds make good police dogs because they are strong, easy to train, and highly motivated. The Suffolk County Police Department Canine Unit on Long Island, New York, uses only male dogs because of their muscular build, body structure, highly acute sense of smell, and temperament. The dogs must be able to obey commands, yet still be very aggressive when necessary. Their strength and speed means that no suspect can outrun or out-muscle them. While Boomer is powerful and relentless, he is also caring, loyal, and loving. Boomer knows not to hurt an innocent person, and when he interacts with kids, he's as gentle as a puppy.

Police dogs like Boomer go through very difficult training in highly specialized facilities. They learn to track everything from suspects and missing people to specific items. They are taught how to stop a criminal from escaping, how to attack, and how to obey their human partner's commands. Officer Mallia explains it in a few words.

Police dogs are trained not to give up.

That's why the attacker could not stop Boomer -- even with a knife.

Boomer knows to think on his own and react appropriately to emergencies. One day, Boomer and Officer Mallia were driving in their patrol car when they saw a suspicious-looking man. He was standing on the side of a house, in the yard. Mallia left Boomer in the car and went to investigate. Mallia asked the man if he owned the house -- and he replied "yes." Mallia didn't trust the man's response or his threatening behavior. The officer demanded to know the house address. If the man was the home owner, as he claimed, he would have no problem giving him the exact numbers.

Unable to respond, the man shoved Mallia to the ground and took off. Mallia pushed a button on his belt and suddenly, the patrol car door swung open. Boomer leaped out and raced after the man. It didn't take long. Within a few minutes, Mallia made the arrest.

Boomer was injured many times during his work. He's been to many places, from suburban neighborhoods and commercial streets to Ground Zero, the site of the 9-11 attacks on the World Trade Center. His heroics have spanned a canine lifetime, from rescuing stolen property, capturing criminals, and finding missing people. While he returned to work after the deadly stabbing, Boomer began to fade. Due to his injuries and advancing age, Boomer was retired to spend his remaining years with Officer Mallia and his family.

Boomer is supposed to enjoy the "good life" now, but he just doesn't see it that way. Mallia reports that every day when he goes to work, Boomer is there "waiting to go with me." A feisty young German shepherd named Blue has taken Boomer's place at work. Boomer now stays home. The retired police dog often visits schools, such as when he met the student authors of this book. The kids loved to meet a real hero who worked so hard to make our community a better place to live.

Boomer Meets The Student-Authors

Boomer visited the kids at school. Most of them were surprised at how gentle and well-behaved he was. They expected a dog that was edgier, more aggressive, and tough to handle. Boomer was a real gentleman!

Officer Mallia introduced the kids to Blue. Blue is Boomer's replacement. Blue was still in training, and very active. He didn't sit still and wasn't very interested in the kids. All he wanted to do was play with Officer Mallia and "attack" the burlap training toy.

At his official retirement ceremony, Boomer received a bone wrapped with a red ribbon. Suffolk County Police Commissioner Richard Dormer commented,

> *I just have to say this is a sad day, believe it or not, that Boomer is leaving us. He's really done a terrific job for officers' safety.*

As a retiree, Boomer is somewhat slower on his paws, and takes longer to respond. Officer Mallia described his old partner's new life.

> *Boomer will be staying home with my wife -- just normal retirement -- eating a lot, gaining weight, much like we're going to do when we get to our retirement age. Boomer has already packed fifteen pounds onto his once-trim seventy-five pound frame. He's been a good dog, and I will sorely miss working with him.*

57

BOOMER'S ART GALLERY

Hero dog *by Brian Smith*

Boomer *by Craig Davide*

Boomer *by Moses Rodriguez*

Boomer gives chase *by Matt Lagueras*

BOOMER BRIEFS

Born: November 12, 1994
Breed: German shepherd
Patrol Certified: July, 1996
Retired: March, 2005

Career Highlights:
*First to reach Brian Petrie, a partially paralyzed
 man trapped under his ATV (All Terrain Vehicle)
*Helped with the recovery effort at the World Trade
 Center after the 9-11 attack
*Was stabbed six times in 2004 at the scene but did not
  back off until suspect was apprehended
*Specializes in Search & Rescue/Cadaver work

Awards:
*Cop of the Year, 1999 and 2003
*Cop of the Month, August 2003
*Top Cop, Suffolk Police Reserves, August 2003
*ASPCA Trooper Award, 2004
*Certificate of Special Recognition, January 2002
*Suffolk Police Reserves Service Award for 9-11
  Recovery Efforts

DANNY *written by:*

| Patricia | Joseph | Skye | Jessica | Doug |

Many people would like to bring their pets to school or college. Imagine the fun everyone would have with a dog in a classroom cafeteria, gym, or dorm room.Of course, bringing pets to school is not permitted, unless you're someone like Tyler Sexton. Wherever Tyler goes, Danny, his dog, is at his side.

The greatest part about having Danny is I get to take my best friend wherever I go.

Tyler is an 18-year old college student at the University of South Florida. He's majoring in biology and hopes to become a doctor. Tyler has more than tests, text books, and difficult classes to deal with -- he was born with cerebral palsy. Cerebral palsy or CP is a neurological disorder that causes motor and physical disabilities. In Tyler's case, he has difficulty with walking, balance, and stability. That's where Danny comes into the picture.

It all began at Denver International Airport. Tyler was returning home after giving a motivational speech. "I speak about cerebral palsy and what God has done for me," Tyler explains. Tyler helps people believe in themselves and what they can accomplish in life. He shows people that with strength and determination, you can overcome the most challenging obstacles thrown in your path.

As he was waiting to board, Tyler noticed a man with a service dog in-training. Tyler struck up a conversation. The man's name was CJ, and he told Tyler about Capable Canines, a program offered by the Guide Dog Foundation. Tyler went home and immediately applied. Seven

60

months later, Danny, a Labrador/golden retriever mix entered his life.

Danny changed my life. He has created opportunities that without him would have been impossible. I love him so much!

The large, gentle Danny was two years old when he met Tyler. Danny was originally trained in New York and then sent to Florida to work with trainer Michael Sargeant. Danny's training was tailored to Tyler's specific needs. After they met, Tyler taught Danny additional maneuvers that would help them negotiate the world as a team.

Danny knows about forty commands, responding only to Tyler's voice. He finds elevators, stairs and locates safe routes so Tyler won't risk falling. When Tyler does lose his balance, Danny braces himself. "He is my railing," Tyler says, "helping me up and down the stairs, in and out of chairs, and weaving through large groups of people."

Danny also picks up dropped objects, executes body blocks in crowds, and stabilizes Tyler as he negotiates steep ascents or descents. Danny is trained to walk alongside Tyler's *Segway*, a motorized transporter that helps Tyler "walk" for long distances.

Danny has dramatically changed Tyler's life. He is his best friend and protector, a constant companion that gives him freedom and independence. "He and I have a special bond," Tyler agrees, "Danny only listens to me and that, in turn, creates an incredible trust between us."

When he's not working, Danny is just like a regular family pet. He loves to play fetch with tennis balls, go to the beach, and swim in the ocean. Danny gets rewarded with small dog biscuits shaped like people. Tyler calls them "people crackers." Danny has a good sense of humor -- Tyler once told him to get his keys and when he returned, Danny had a bag of tennis balls in his mouth.

Portrait of Danny
by Jessica Pollock

Some people and dogs do a single, heroic act. Other people and dogs are heroic every day, in the small, routine things they do for others. Danny is that kind of hero, staying at Tyler's side when they work, and next to him when it's time to hang out.

FAITH written by:

Katie   Brian   Matthew   Julia

Working dogs can be trained to do just about anything. They can open doors, guide visually impaired people, partner with canine police, and serve as "ears" for the hearing disabled. How many of them can dial 911 in an emergency?

Leana Beasley had been in a coma for two months. When she recovered, Leana was left with multiple disabilities and health issues. The Richland, Washington, resident decided that a service dog would help her live a more active and independent life. Her first service dog was a rottweiler mix named Bronson. He was Leana's "partner" for ten years. Although Bronson still lives with Leana, he was retired because of age-related problems. Then Faith entered Leana's life.

Faith is a purebred rottweiler. The breeder, Anna Nichols, nicknamed the puppy "Miss Personality" because she was so smart, learned quickly, and loved to be with people. Faith went to live with Leana, Michael, Leana's 20-year old son, Bronson, Tiger the cat, and Tangy, the parrot. Leana decided that she would train the reddish-gold, playful puppy by herself.

Leana knew what she was doing. First, she took the puppy's name from a bible verse that says, "Faith is the substance of things hoped for, the evidence of things not seen." The dog went beyond all of Leana's hopes, completely devoting herself to her disabled owner. Ironically, many people mistakenly believe that rottweilers are vicious. Faith proves them all wrong -- she loves children and is friendly to everyone. Leana explains:

There is no such thing as a bad breed of dog. There are only bad owners. When any puppy is born it's innocent and helpless . . . bad owners don't spend enough time with their puppies, don't train them properly, and sometimes physically abuse them. A good dog owner can take any breed of dog and raise it to be a gentle, well-trained dog who loves everybody.

Leana spent a lot of time working with Faith, training her to assist in medical emergencies.

Teaching a dog to do something that requires a lot of skill. It is like building a long chain. You have to teach each "link" of the chain, one at a time.

For example, to open a door, you must have a lever handle. A cord is tied to the handle, and the dog learns to grab the cord in her mouth, pull down, and back up. If there is a lock, the dog must first know how to push with her nose. You need a lock button that makes it possible. The button is painted a color that the dog can see. Once the dog learns those things, she needs to put everything together and know that to open the door she has to push the button and then pull on the handle.

Many of these behaviors are essential in dealing with medical emergencies. When Leana sleeps she is hooked up to machines that help her breathe. Without the machines, Leana could stop breathing completely. If there's trouble, alarms sound, and Faith is trained to wake Leana up. If Leana doesn't wake up, Faith pulls off the mask on her face and dials 911.

A dog who can dial 911? One of the most inconceivable canine rescues took place in October. Leana was feeling sick all day. Faith had been staying very close to her, never leaving the space near her wheelchair. Faith, as with many medical service dogs, can smell chemical changes in the body. Faith knew that something was very wrong.

Suddenly, Leana lost consciousness and fell out of her wheelchair.

Faith could not wake her. The dog raced to the telephone and followed Leana's training, using her nose to push the large button that speed-dialed 911. Faith barked loudly as soon as she heard the dispatcher's voice. Leana described the telephone call.

Faith barked and talked into the phone every time the dispatcher talked. This was the very first time that Faith has ever had to use these skills in a real life and death situation. Faith did it with accuracy and precision.

Perhaps equally amazing, was the fact that the dispatcher guessed what was happening. Jenny Buchanan didn't know that Faith was a medical service dog trained to dial 911. She figured that something was very wrong, and the police should be notified.

Police Officer Scott Morrell was sent to Leana's home. Like Jenny, he had no experience with a medical service dog. Faith opened the lock, and then the door, using her mouth. Suddenly, Morrell faced a large rottweiler staring at him. There was no way to know whether the dog was friendly, or trained to be an attack dog.

Portrait of Faith
by Michael Mascaro

Officer Morrell was not sure what to do. He believed that most rottweilers were dangerous, ready to attack intruders. It was a very tense moment. Morrell took a chance that the dog was trying to tell him that something was very wrong. He made the first move, entering Leana's home. Faith stood back, following her training. Morell searched the house and quickly found Leana. He called an ambulance and Leana was rushed to the hospital. "I was in the hospital for three weeks," Leana reports, "pretty weak and sick." She was suffering from a liver problem that prevented her body from utilizing critical medication. Without Faith, Leana might not be alive today to tell the story of her heroic working dog.

For The Love Of Service

A service dog is a lot more than a family pet. According to the Americans with Disabilities Act (ADA, 1990), a service dog is "individually trained to do work or perform tasks for the benefit of a person with a disability." Disability is defined as any "mental or physical condition which substantially limits a major life activity." Federal law protects the rights of disabled people to bring their service dogs into public places.

Service dogs are used to help people with problems in:

seeing
hearing
walking
speaking
breathing
balance
performing manual tasks
self-care
learning
working
medical conditions such as seizures
psychiatric conditions

ROSELLE *written by:*

| Craig | Kevin | Brandon | Matt |

September 11, 2001. It began as just another working day. Michael Hingson went to his office on the 78th floor of the north tower in the World Trade Center. He got to his desk and started work.

Suddenly, there was an explosion. Chunks of fiery debris rained outside the window. The building swayed, and the smell of jet fuel filled the air. Michael could hear the panic, smell the fumes, and feel the motion of the building.

He could not see anything because Michael Hingson has been blind since birth.

Michael began working with guide dogs at a very young age. He received his first dog from Guide Dogs for the Blind in San Rafael, California. He was only 14 years old at the time. Since then, Michael has worked with a total of five guide dogs. Michael explains:

I can request a certain type of dog, but mostly I ask for a dog with a certain personality. I like friendly dogs, but they also must know when they can visit and when they must work. So, I didn't really ask for Roselle by name, but she fit perfectly my requests for the attributes I wanted in a guide dog.

Roselle was born on the Guide Dogs for the Blind campus in California. At eight weeks old she went to live with "puppy raisers" Kay and Ted Stern -- 300 miles from her birthplace. The puppy raisers taught

Roselle how to live in a community, go into public places, and fly on airplanes. "The puppies learn that they must behave while out in public," adds Michael.

Roselle returned to San Rafael for five months of training. "Then I met her and our relationship began," says Michael. The most important thing was for both of them to learn how to work together. It takes trust from both members of the team to be successful.

I trust her with my life, Michael says, and she also trusts me with hers. It is important to explain that we must each trust the other. I believe it takes a year to fully develop the bond and two-way trust that makes a good guide dog team work.

Michael and Roselle at the World Trade Center

When his job moved to New York, Michael and Roselle went as a team. One of the first things they did in the new office was to learn their way around. The two of them explored the north tower. Sometimes they got lost. "Getting lost," observes Michael, "is the best way to learn something." They found their way when Michael asked questions and gave Roselle specific commands like forward, left, and right.

On 9-11, Roselle was sleeping under Michael's desk when the World Trade Center was attacked. The airplane hit about 15 floors above them. They had to make their way down 78 flights of stairs to survive. Michael describes their roles.

Roselle was trained to perform the task of guiding. Roselle's job is to be the pilot of the team. My job is to be the navigator.

Together, Michael and Roselle made their way to the stairs. Michael had to remain in charge. He knew where to go and carefully instructed Roselle with the commands she knew. It was all teamwork.

They reached the stairwell and headed down. The air got thicker and hotter, filled with the stench of jet fuel fumes. The crowds got larger, with people moving quickly, but not in a panic or stampede.

Michael and Roselle were at the 50th floor when the second plane

Portrait of Roselle
by Patrick Greene

rammed into the south tower.

Suddenly, people were bumping into Michael. They were going the wrong way. "I heard applause and was told they were firefighters," Michael recalls. "I clapped a few on the back, but I was scared for where they were going."

It took an hour to get out of the north tower -- 50 minutes on the stairs and another ten minutes to make it through the lobby. As they burst through the doors, and down the street, the second tower collapsed. Michael recalls it vividly.

It sounded like a metal and concrete waterfall.

A rolling gray cloud of ash, glass, and debris raced towards them. A woman near them could not see because her eyes were filled with soot. Michael took her arm, and Roselle guided both of them. Cries of terror pierced the air, and they ran for their lives. Yet Roselle was able to concentrate, and Michael kept the commands simple.

The world turned gray around them, covered in the remains of what had once been two, 110-story buildings. Everyone had turned gray as well, coated with ash and soot. Roselle looked like a gray Labrador retriever. Even people with perfect eyesight couldn't see more than six inches ahead of them. Breathing became increasingly difficult.

That cloud of debris of dirt and junk and garbage in the air
was so thick that we were breathing in more particles than air.

In one of the most amazing stories of teamwork, both Michael and Roselle survived the horrific attacks. Roselle received many awards for her work on that day. Today, they still continue their relationship based on trust, teamwork, and devotion.

Roselle is a regular member of our family, Michael says.
She makes me feel safe, confident, and happy that I am alive.

Search and rescue operations after the collapse of The
World Trade Center

 There were many heroes, human and canine, on 9-11 and in the aftermath of the terrorist attacks. More than two hundred and fifty search and rescue dogs worked around the clock at the Pentagon and the World Trade Center. They searched tirelessly for survivors, cadavers, and human remains. The dogs had no gas masks or protective clothing. They worked, breathing the dust and debris of what remained after the attacks. They climbed and searched places considered far too dangerous for humans. They did not stop, until one-by-one, their handlers took them home.

PAWS TO RECOGNIZE™

NAME:
Gentle Ben

HOME:
Vancouver, Washington

ORGANIZATION:
Delta Society Pet Partners®

NAME:
Trouble

HOME:
Miami, Florida

ORGANIZATION:
Customs and Border
Protection

Heroes come in all shapes and sizes!

Canine heroes may look, sound, and play very different from one another. They come from around the world, and show courage, dedication, and loyalty. The dogs all have one thing in common -- they work to help people everyday.

The Paws to Recognize program seeks to honor these amazing canine heroes. Humans are invited to vote for the dog they believe should win the honor. The top-voted candidates are invited to leave their paw prints in cement, as part of the Hollywood-style Canine Heroes Walk of Fame.

Meet two Paws To Recognize heroes:

Gentle Ben and Trouble.

Trouble (left) meets Gentle Ben.

GENTLE BEN *written by:*

Jonathan   **Ashley**   **Moses**   **Eugene**   **Eric**

Portrait of Gentle Ben
by Alex Kantor

No one seemed surprised by the 165-pound Newfoundland sitting in the front row at a funeral. Gentle Ben, that special Newfoundland, was saying good-bye to his friend, Larry.

Larry had been head of security at the hospital where Ben and his owner, Pat Dowell, visited every Thursday. Before he died, Larry had asked his minister to make sure that Pat and Ben sat in the front row with his family.

When the minister introduced Pat and Ben, there were huge gasps, oohs, and ahhs. Many had not seen a Newfoundland, but had the same love of animals as Larry. The minister spoke highly of the therapy work that Ben and others do, and how, like Ben, Larry was so gentle.

Pat and the others at the funeral cried for Larry. Big, Gentle Ben was sad and silent. He could not cry with tears because dogs show their emotions in very different ways. Pat said it best:

Larry loved Ben and Ben loved Larry.

Larry's daughter's family, who had met Ben in the past, came in before the funeral and saw Pat and Ben already seated. It was very comforting for them to see Ben in their time of need.

Each week, Ben and Larry had a special play routine in the hospital lobby. Nobody wanted to miss the weekly "Ben and Larry Show" where Larry would hide, and then peek around a corner, waiting for the dog's response. Larry would whistle -- a signal Ben knew immediately. The dog would dodge back and forth pulling Pat along with him. All of a sudden, Ben would find Larry and there was a burst of high fives and cookies.

Pat and Gentle Ben are a therapy dog team from Vancouver, Washington. They live with Jeff, Pat's husband, and 17-year old Misty the cat. Larry's hospital is one of the many places they visit for humane causes, helping people feel better, and refocusing their lives.

Gentle Ben got his name because he looks and acts like a sweet, giant brown teddy bear -- a natural for pet assisted therapy with the Delta Society Pet Partners Program. Pet assisted therapy is a growing service field that uses trained human-animal teams as integral parts of a patient's treatment plan to help promote recovery. Gentle Ben and Pat began their therapy work together in the Clark County juvenile justice system. The use of therapy dog teams in prison has increased over the years, and correction experts have discovered that animals have a calming, beneficial effect on inmates.

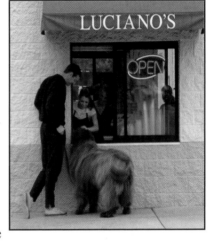

Many of the young people are left isolated and lonely after being incarcerated for committing crimes. Some kids have to testify against abusive parents, appearing in a terrifying courtroom environment. Big-hearted Gentle Ben is always there to support them. Deborah Wood, a local reporter, writes:

Because of Ben's pioneering work, other programs linking therapy dogs with juvenile offenders have started in the state.

Gentle Ben brings light into often dreary lives. The kids are frequently sad, angry, hostile, and violent. They're struggling with a childhood scarred by abuse, neglect, and every form of aggression and carnage imaginable. Pat, using her degree in criminology, worked with

73

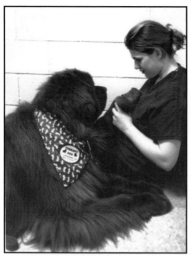

Ben at work in the juvenile detention center.

the Clark County system to develop a pet assisted therapy program designed to help the kids feel better about themselves, change their attitudes, hearts, and minds, and lift their spirits to enable them to emotionally and psychologically survive incarceration.

Ben's first job in the juvenile detention center was with a young girl going through very rough times. She was abused and abandoned by her family and consequently committed several crimes. Ben helped build her self-esteem, and gave her the courage to face the problems of living in jail. During the 18 months they worked with her, Ben and Pat took on the role of family. Instinctively, Ben knew how to comfort people who were in physical or emotional pain.

Gentle Ben and Pat's work expanded from the juvenile detention center to Larry's hospital, and into schools. Pat describes the process:

Ben and I went through the pet assisted training program to become certified as a team because of the gentle nature of Newfoundland dogs in general and Ben, specifically. Ben loves visiting the various places we go for his therapy work because he gets lots of attention. He loves to pull his cart and give rides to children because when he's finished, the kids come to pet him and give him treats.

Even when Gentle Ben is playing, he helps people. When one of Ben's best friends died, a Bernese mountain dog named Breese, Pat and several other therapy dog teams decided to start an annual canine memorial birthday party. Instead of gifts for the dogs, people bring school supplies and clothing for the pre-school

Gentle Ben pulling the cart he uses to take kids for a ride.

children at the local YWCA where Breese visited. Last year, eighty-five people and thirty dogs attended the party.

Gentle Ben was awarded the prestigious *Pedigree's Paws To Recognize* award as a top-voted USA service dog. He went to New York City, received a medal, and had his paw prints enshrined in cement as part of the "Canine Heroes Walk of Fame."

With all the celebrity, Gentle Ben and Pat's goals remain simple: to bring a minimum of 100 smiles a week. That's over 5000 smiles a year, quite an undertaking for a shaggy brown Newfoundland.

Gentle Ben's love and kindness make a difference in so many lives. Perhaps Deborah Wood said it best, when she wrote about Gentle Ben,

> *Hero dogs earn their reputation one day at a time,*
> *just like human heroes.*

TROUBLE *written by:*

| James | Nick | Bobby | Timmy |

The results are in! Trouble has been voted one of the top service dogs in the United States. Americans can sleep easier knowing that we have a 31 pound beagle guarding Miami International Airport against agro-terrorism.

Trouble is a seven-year old beagle who works for the Department of Homeland Security, customs' parent agency. The U.S. Customs and Border Protection (CBP) is the largest federal canine enforcement agency in the country. CPB canine teams are assigned to more than 73 ports of entry and 82 border patrol stations throughout the United States. The U.S. borders, land ports, seaports, international airports, and mail facilities must be guarded. Canine Officer Sherrie Ann Keblish and her partner, Trouble, are one of 1100 special detector teams.

Portrait
by James Levine

Some dog teams are trained to detect chemicals that are used in weapons. Other dogs sniff out explosives that could be hidden in cargo or luggage. There are also currency teams that can detect the odor of money being smuggled out of the U.S. When people try to enter the country illegally, there are detector dogs trained to find hidden people. Teams with search and rescue dogs are trained to find missing people. Narcotics detector dogs find drugs such as marijuana, heroin, cocaine, and other illegal substances.

76

These canines do amazing things. A dog can effectively examine a car in five to six minutes when it would take a human at least 20 minutes. Dogs can sniff out terrorists, explosives, smuggled currency, concealed people and narcotics in minutes, compared to humans who have to open and examine each piece of baggage. The most important qualities in these dogs are their acute sense of smell, gentle nature, ability to stay calm in crowded, noisy places, and a strong food drive. When choosing these special dogs, their breed isn't the most important factor. Most of the dogs are from animal shelters, humane societies, and rescue leagues. The main requirements are to have the right personality and enthusiasm for retrieving objects.

Miami International Airport has seven beagle canine teams. Their job is to detect fruits, vegetables, meats, and other prohibited items that can carry dangerous animals, pests, or plant diseases with the potential to seriously harm U.S. agriculture. Last year, these canine teams accounted for almost 6200 positive seizures, which could have cost billions of dollars in damage.

When it comes to enthusiasm and accuracy in his specialty, Trouble leads the pack! Trouble came from an animal shelter in Texas, and received nearly 13 weeks of training at the National Detector Dog Training Center in Orlando, Florida. In 2001, he teamed up with Officer Sherrie and started working. Sherrie explains how Trouble works.

Trouble's job is very rewarding. He views his work as a game.
He enjoys playing the game and plays hard at it everyday.

Trouble begins his day at 3:30 A.M. He sleeps in a kennel just south of the airport. He loves to bark at the local wildlife -- raccoons, peacocks, and foxes. When Trouble hears the sound of Sherrie's car, he barks to greet her. It's time to go to work.

Trouble and Sherrie head for the airport to work between 8 to 12 flights a day. They will inspect passengers, baggage, mail and carry-ons. Trouble sniffs for the specific prohibited fruits, vegetables, meats, and animal by-products that could introduce foreign pests or diseases. He also

Portrait of Trouble
by Bobby Iorizzo

sniffs for meat products to keep the United States free from Foot and Mouth Disease and Mad Cow Disease. There are 50 distinct odors that Trouble has been trained to find.

Sometimes Trouble works at the mail facility checking through boxes and packages of registered and express international mail as they move along on a treadmill-type machine. Trouble and Sherrie also weave through passengers and baggage, with the beagle's nose hard at work. Trouble is trained to sit if he finds anything suspicious. When that happens, Sherrie swings into action, informing the passengers of a canine "alert," and asking if there are any agricultural items in their bags. The items can be as innocent as a piece of fruit or melon in a passenger's lunch bag, or as serious as smuggled animals or agricultural materials. Either way, it can lead to a potential disaster.

Perhaps one of Trouble's most dramatic saves was when he detected a piece of fruit in an international passenger's lunch bag. Unknown to the passenger, the fruit carried over 20 larvae of Mediterranean fruit fly, one of the world's most destructive pests. It had the potential to destroy the entire citrus crop in the state of Florida.

Every case is handled differently. Officer Sherrie explains.

Items are usually seized and destroyed unless they're
birds or protected wildlife which are confiscated.

and put into a quarantine area for a certain time
period . . . individuals who try to smuggle something illegal
can also be fined and face legal prosecution.

Trouble's heroic work has been recognized in many ways. He has appeared on *National Fox News* and *Friends, Univision, Animal Planet,* and local stations in New York City and Miami. He goes to schools and trade shows to demonstrate his skills. He has traveled to different airports, met officials and celebrities, stayed in pet friendly hotels and eaten in New York City restaurants. Trouble received *Pedigree's Paws To Recognize* award and traveled to New York to receive a medal and his paw prints enshrined in cement as part of the "Canine Heroes Walk." Thanks to the dedication of detector teams like Trouble and Officer Sherrie Keblish, Americans stay healthier and safer.

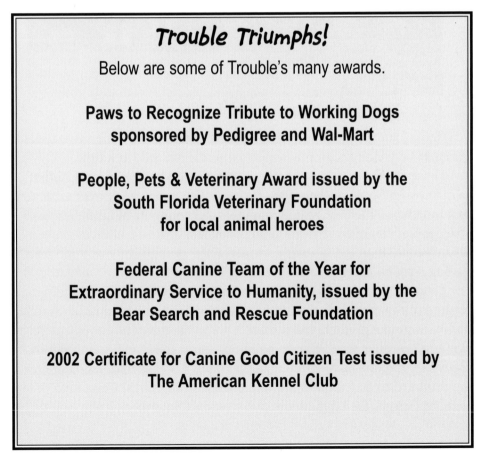

Trouble Triumphs!

Below are some of Trouble's many awards.

**Paws to Recognize Tribute to Working Dogs
sponsored by Pedigree and Wal-Mart**

**People, Pets & Veterinary Award issued by the
South Florida Veterinary Foundation
for local animal heroes**

**Federal Canine Team of the Year for
Extraordinary Service to Humanity, issued by the
Bear Search and Rescue Foundation**

**2002 Certificate for Canine Good Citizen Test issued by
The American Kennel Club**

Great Dog Stories

Heroes and greatness go hand-in-hand. Sometimes both move quietly through the years, accomplishing great feats, one step at a time.

These stories are about people and dogs that have made a difference in our world. Some of them, like Bide-A-Wee, reach back over a century to a time when there were no computers, no commercial airplanes, and few people who even *thought* about homeless animals. Certainly, even fewer people than today, ever considered the possibility that "one man's garbage can be another man's treasure."

Then there are those who saw the human service potential in dogs, leading to organizations that train dogs who are almost human in their ability to guide, predict, and protect. Of course, many of our pets quietly perform a similar service as companions, protectors, and loving family members. Experts have speculated that "new" breeds, like labradoodles, are designed to fulfill these important roles in our lives. Certainly, without Gizmo, the labradoodle, we wouldn't have *The Gizmo Tales*!

BIDE-A-WEE *written by:*

Kelly

Dayna

Adam

Kyle

Mrs. Kibbe

Paris is known for fashion, art, culture, and history. Visitors love to shop, dine, and take in the sights. Some visitors discover unexpected things in this romantic city.

Mrs. Flora D'Auby Jenkins Kibbe was one of them.

During the turn of the 19th century, Mrs. Kibbe was visiting Paris when she encountered the *Barrone I'Herpents* dog refuge. It was a unique humane group whose mission was to find stray and unwanted dogs. The group used a small Renault ambulance to search the streets of Paris for these animals. What made them so unique was that they kept and cared for the animals instead of destroying them, as customary for that era. The dogs were sheltered until the refuge could find them new homes.

Mrs. Kibbe returned to her home in New York City, determined to bring the concept stateside. She chose the name "Bide-A-Wee" because it was a popular phrase in Scotland that meant "stay awhile." Her goal was to expand the humane mission to include every kind of stray animal, from dogs and cats, to horses and farm animals. In addition, Bide-A-Wee placed and maintained fresh water troughs throughout the city streets. The drinking water was for the many carriage and riding horses that were the main means of transportation in those days.

By 1909, Mrs. Kibbe was housing almost 200 dogs in "makeshift"

82

quarters. She lived in a fancy, Lexington Avenue neighborhood, and people were getting annoyed over the constant barking and mess. To avoid further community problems, Mrs. Kibbe quickly set up a temporary Bide-A-Wee country shelter in New Jersey.

Eventually, it settled into a permanent home on 38th Street right near the East River in New York. Today, Bide-A-Wee still maintains its

original mission with cats, dogs, kittens, and puppies. Joan Stoppa, Education and Outreach Manager explains.

Bide A-Wee gives dogs a "second chance" to find responsible and loving homes. Many more wonderful, innocent animals would lose their lives in today's throwaway society if there weren't places like us to help them find a person or family suited to their personalities.

Joan Stoppa

Bide-A-Wee also has a shelter in Westhampton, veterinary clinics, and "Golden Years Retirement Home" for older dogs and cats left behind by their owners' death or serious illness. Stoppa adds,

As a non-profit organization, Bide-A-Wee shows us that love is not measured in dollars and that companion animals give so much and ask for so little.

Since it began, Bide-A-Wee has found homes for more than 1 million pets! Each year, Bide-A-Wee finds homes for 5000 animals and provides life-saving veterinary care for 35,000 pets. Most people don't realize that almost 25 percent of the shelter dogs are pure breeds. The most common animals in the shelter are large, mixed breed dogs and domestic short-haired cats.

Many of the animals brought to Bide-A-Wee are from guardians or owners who can no longer care for their pets. Some of the reasons include allergies in the family, an older person

Chinese Crested rescued dog
by Kyle Vadnais

Bide-A-Wee
Reading to Dogs Program,
Claire Vandewart
with Jedi and Calypso

who has become ill, health problems, or the death of the owner. Other people move and their new home won't allow pets. Worst of all are those people who just lose interest in their pet and don't want it any more. Bide-A-Wee doesn't pick up stray animals or accept ones that have been found on the street. Those animals go to the town shelters, so that the animals at Bide-A-Wee remain safe, healthy, and ready for adoption.

Bide-A-Wee also runs many special events and educational outreach programs. These include *Reading to Dogs* (to help children improve reading skills), outreach programs that bring pets to schools, hospitals, and nursing homes, bereavement counseling for individuals who have lost a pet, and *Seniors Adopt Free* (to match senior citizens with adult dogs and cats).

Stoppa talks about the experience of working at the shelter:

Bide-A-Wee therapy dog

Bide-A-Wee rescued dog
by Kyle Vadnais

My favorite parts about working at Bide-A-Wee are the wonderful animals I get to know and the interesting and generous people I meet in the different facets of my work. I think of these pets and their guardians (the staff and volunteers at Bide-A-Wee) as "heroes" because they are bringing so much love and happiness.

Bide-A-Wee Beginnings

GUIDE DOG FOUNDATION

written by:

| Patrick | Krystin | Anthony | Jessica | Zachary |

Mrs. Dorothy Harrison Eustis, ca. 1904-1924

Mrs. Dorothy Harrison Eustis had a good life as a wealthy American living in Switzerland. Eustis devoted most of her time to breeding her favorite dog, the German shepherd. She had developed an excellent reputation as a breeder and training expert by working with the Swiss Army, and various city police departments throughout Europe. Eustis was determined to demonstrate the intelligence, loyalty, and trainability of German shepherds. The last thing she wanted was cheap publicity, or people clamoring for puppies.

When Eustis was invited to write an article for the *Saturday Evening Post,* she made a decision that would eventually change the lives of thousands of people. Instead of writing about herself, she wrote about her visit to a school in Potsdam, Germany, where German shepherds were being trained to guide veterans who had been blinded in World War I. In a 1927 edition, she wrote "The Seeing Eye," an article detailing personal observations of the extraordinary intelligence and fidelity of the German shepherd in rehabilitation of the blind. Eustis described how the dogs learned to think while maintaining strict obedience. They behaved as partners, not as machines. She discussed the stages of learning and problem-solving that made the dogs into worthy citizens, providing happiness,

companionship, and independence for their guardians. With a "seeing eye" dog at a person's side, miracles happened. Suddenly blind people could lead normal lives, even secure jobs. They didn't have to be dependent on friends and family members for all their needs.

Morris Frank, a young, blind man living in Nashville, Tennessee, heard about the article. Morris Frank had lost the use of his eyes in two separate accidents, and hated how he was forced to depend on other people. Eustis' seeing eye dogs sounded like the answer to his wildest dreams. Frank contacted Eustis and asked her if she would train a seeing eye dog for him. She agreed, but only if he came to Switzerland for the training.

In 1928 Frank traveled to Switzerland to meet Buddy, a specially trained dog from Eustis' kennels. Frank spent a lot of time, energy, and dedication learning how to work with Buddy. The results went beyond his greatest expectations. Frank and Buddy quickly became the first American guide dog team.

When Frank returned to Nashville, he and Buddy received a lot of publicity. Imagine what people thought when they saw a dog guiding a blind man through the streets! Few had ever witnessed such a sight. Suddenly, many blind people wanted guide dogs for themselves. In 1929 Eustis returned to the United States to help Frank establish a seeing eye dog training school in Nashville. Using $10,000 donated by Eustis, Frank set up the first official guide dog school in America. It was called *The Seeing Eye*, after Eustis' original article. The first class had two students. By the end of the first year, a total of 17 people had experienced new-found freedom with seeing eye dogs by their sides.

Guide Dog Foundation
by Patrick Greene

Years later, a group of civic leaders decided to establish a school in the New York metropolitan area. Their goal was to offer seeing eye or guide dogs, without charging the recipient for costly breeding, boarding, and training services. In 1946 they set up the Guide Dog Foundation as "Guiding Eyes, Inc." They hired William

Guide dog team
by Krystin White

Holzmann, a dog trainer, to develop a training method. The headquarters was located in a small space in Forest Hills, New York. Two people graduated in the first year. Growing quickly, the new organization purchased land in Smithtown, New York, and in 1949, the name was changed to the Guide Dog Foundation for the Blind, Inc.

The Smithtown headquarters expanded rapidly. A kennel was built, and students stayed in local rooming houses. Mr. Holzmann trained the dogs in strings -- groups of six to eight. In the 1960's they began a breeding program with Labrador retrievers and golden retrievers -- moving away from the popular German shepherds. Many of the guide dogs that work today are decendents of those original dogs. The demand for guide dogs and training was constantly increasing.

Today, guide dogs hold a very special status. They are permitted, *by law*, into all public areas including hotels, restaurants, theaters, stores, parks, gyms, and schools. They ride in all forms of public transportation, including buses, trains, and airplanes. The Americans With Disabilities Act, passed in 1992, assures that no one can deny a disabled person, with his or her service dog, access to public areas. Clearly, the law recognized the rights of disabled people to lead full, independent lives.

The Guide Dog Foundation continues to provide guide dogs free of charge to blind and visually impaired people seeking independence and flexibility in their lives. Students come to the Smithtown campus from all over the United States and the world. They meet and train with their new dogs. Classes are small, and individualized instruction helps create new service teams.

The Smithtown campus looks a lot different than when it opened in the 1940's. It now

Devera Lynn,
Communications Director
Guide Dog Foundation

Bruno, guide dog and
Freddy, guide dog puppy

includes administration offices, student residences, state-of-the art kennels, a puppy nursery, obstacle course and a tranquil Japanese garden. The Foundation offers public education to broaden understanding of vision, visual impairment, blindness, and disability rights.

The process has changed as well. The puppies are born and whelped at the puppy nursery on the Smithtown campus. When they're seven to eight weeks old, they go to special families who act as foster homes. The families, called "puppy walkers" socialize the future guide dogs, teach them basic obedience, and give them the love and attention needed for their work. Devera Lynn, Communications Director at the Guide Dog Foundation, describes what happens when the puppies are old enough to return to Smithtown.

Puppies generally return from the puppy walkers to the Guide Dog Foundation at about twelve to fourteen months old. They begin formal guide dog training which lasts approximately three to six months. Our guide dogs are bred for temperament, gentleness, intelligence and physical soundness. They are taught how to find and follow a clear path, maneuver around obstacles, and stop at curbs when it is unsafe to proceed.

Heidi Vandewinckel, CSW
Chair of the Board of Directors
Guide Dog Foundation
and her guide dog, Bruno

Not all of the dogs pass the final test to become a guide dog. There are many reasons why a dog is not selected, such as being too timid or friendly, too easily distracted, or have even minor health problems that would be difficult for a blind person to handle. Devera describes what happens to these already trained dogs.

89

If a dog does not make it as a guide, they may go into our Capable Canine program. Capable Canines are trained to assist people with disabilities other than sight related. Sometimes the dogs transfer into programs such as Alcohol, Tobacco, and Firearms (search and rescue dogs), police dogs, therapy dogs, and facility dogs.

When the guide dogs complete their training and pass their tests, they are each carefully matched with a student. Students and their dogs bond and learn how to work together as a team. Each class consists of ten students and their dogs, and two instructors. Blind students must first practice the commands that the dog already knows. In addition, they learn proper canine care, and the laws that protect their dog's right to be allowed in public places. In order to learn how to work as a team, students begin with leash guiding, and then move on to visit nearby towns, country roads, city streets, shopping malls, stores, and public transportation. It takes 25 days to train a new guide dog team!

The Foundation has successfully educated hearing-impaired people who are blind, as well as those who are physically challenged, to handle their guide dogs. It costs a total of $30,000 to complete the training of just one guide dog! The Guide Dog Foundation guarantees that all their students receive these services completely free of charge.

After graduation, the foundation maintains regular communication with its graduates, offering assistance and services.

Guide dog puppy
by Kaitlyn Emory

Craig's Story

   As a resident of West Palm Beach, Florida, my community was hit with a series devastating hurricanes. During this time I received several concerned telephone calls from the Guide Dog Foundation, to make sure everything was okay. I was really impressed by the care shown from the staff, to ensure the safety of all of the graduates in the region. They asked about my guide dog Wilson, and how he was holding up. I was pleased to report that he was doing very well, and that the storms didn't even faze him. His guiding was impeccable.

   My home is in an adjoining community to my job at the Veterans Administration. We walk about one-half mile every day, which is usually uneventful. But the conditions changed dramatically after the hurricanes. Wilson was completely undeterred. He maneuvered with ease around tree branches and limbs, as well as piles of debris. Whenever we reached a block in the path, he would stop, think about the best route around it, and then proceed. It was remarkable! Wilson knew that it was his job to get me to work safely. He was in his glory; he really took on the role of a great guide dog.

   While Wilson protected me from these unknown elements, the Guide Dog Foundation offered their services. Because we lost power and it was difficult to gain access to transportation, staff made trips to deliver fresh drinking water and dog food to myself and other graduates. I never imagined that the aftercare services offered by the school would include this kind of attention. I am very grateful.

HARLEY *written by:*

Nadia　　　　**James**　　　　**Alyssa**　　　　**Dean**

Harley sends a powerful message: one man's garbage is another man's treasure. It should be the caption under Harley's photograph. As a ten-month old puppy wandering the streets of Amityville, New York, he was brought to the Town of Babylon Animal Shelter. Most prospective owners are not too fond of pit bull types, especially large dogs. This 75 pound boxer/American bulldog mix, had been at the shelter for six weeks, and no one wanted him.

Liz in her grooming shop,
Grooming Unlimited

Liz Rock, owner of Grooming Unlimited in Huntington, New York, was at the shelter hoping to find a small dog for her friend. She couldn't find one. Liz recalls her search:

I asked to walk through the rest of the shelter not knowing my life was about to change.

At home, Liz already had a "full house," with three Yorkies, a Pomeranian, a cockatoo, a Persian cat, and a cat that was rescued from a dog carrier thrown into a dumpster. It was her *friend* who wanted a dog -- yet Liz couldn't resist.

He sat there looking a lot like Petey from the Little Rascals. *The patch on the eye did it.*

92

Before she was fully aware of what she was doing, Liz asked to take the dog out and test his behavior.

He seemed to be a very happy boy as if saying, "Let's go home, momma."

Liz named the dog Harley because she loves to ride motorcycles. Harley now stands taller than a golden retriever, has floppy ears, and is mostly white with a tan patch around one eye, and several spots sprinkled on his body. She couldn't resist his personality.

Portrait of Harley
by Alyssa Goldberg

Harley is always happy and thrilled to meet people; his tongue is always looking to lick you.

Liz discovered that Harley was mistreated as a puppy. If you lift a newspaper too fast, Harley gets scared. He also has a small hole in his trachea (wind pipe) that came from a prong collar. He was probably lifted off the ground by his leash, and the prong collar punctured his trachea. Sometimes the puncture leads to a cough -- a condition that will probably grow worse over time. Harley, like many dogs, has had an odd reaction to the abuse he suffered. Liz explains:

Some dogs, when they have been abused, only love that much more when they find their forever home.

Harley went farther than most rescued dogs to prove his trust. Liz's friend Sue owns a clothing line for dogs called *Waggin' Wear*. As soon as Sue saw Harley, she knew he was a hit. Harley soon started modeling for *Waggin' Wear*, posing for photo shoots. He was noticed, and subsequently invited to audition for a commercial in New York City. The rescued dog beat out all the pros at the audition, and was hired for a Burger King commercial promoting the *Cat in the Hat* movie. They began filming the commercial on October 17th -- the two year anniversary of what Liz calls, "gotcha day," or the day she met Harley at

Portrait of Harley
by James Raheb

the shelter. Harley was fitted for his Dr. Seuss outfit, and Liz handled him during the one-and-one-half day shoot. Harley didn't work for doggie treats like the pros -- he did everything for fun, and because he trusted Liz.

Harley works best with love, not stern commands.

Harley makes a difference wherever he goes. The boy who appeared in the commercial with Harley was afraid of dogs. Harley showed the boy that there was nothing scary about him. At the end of the shoot, all the people on the set applauded Harley.

The commercial aired on several networks. Harley also appeared at the Woodhull Elementary School to show his commercial off, in celebration of Dr. Seuss Day. The kids loved everything about Harley. At the Babylon Town Shelter, Harley led "Cat in the Hat Day" to promote adopting animals from the shelter. The event was overwhelmingly successful. Harley showed up with a very personal message. Every wag of his tail seemed to say, "I came from here and look where I ended up." Liz advises:

Just give a pet a chance. If you think of the shelter as an orphanage, you will realize that no one asks to go there, and everyone is hoping for a better life.

Harley shows everyone how important it is not to give up. He sat in that cage for six weeks, never knowing if he would be put down or brought to a new home. It was literally life or death. Suddenly, everything changed. Harley went from homeless to television.

Harley still goes to work with Liz everyday. Her customers frequently tell her how they would love to take Harley home with them. Liz laughs.

Maybe your Harley is waiting for you right now at the shelter!

Harley's Pin-up Page
Compliments of Viewpoints Photography

Ellen and Bobby's Story

written by:

| Stephanie | Alex | Robert | Justine |

Heroes come in all shapes and sizes. This is a story about four heroes -- two dogs and two people, who had never met before the fateful day that brought them together. For a moment in time, these people and dogs worked together, proving that not only is dog man's best friend, but man is also dog's best friend.

It was August, and Ellen and Bobby were enjoying the sun. Ellen was hesitant to go boating, but Bobby was very convincing.

The tide is coming in, and I'll put the boat away unless you come with me.

The daylight was beginning to fade in the late afternoon sun. It was too beautiful a day to end. Ellen recalls the moment, never knowing that her decision was a life-and-death choice.

I wasn't planning to go, but then changed my mind in the end.

At about the same time, a father, his two daughters, and two big standard poodles decided to set out in their boat. As the shoreline faded away, they thought it would be great fun to go swimming. They jumped

96

into the water and started to play, unaware that their boat began to drift. No one was wearing a life jacket. Before long, the strong current had pushed their boat far away, separating the father from his daughters. They could not reach one another!

The family called for help from the boats passing by, but the wind was strong and noisy so no one heard them. The family and the boat drifted further apart.

The girls were tiring, the water pulling them under. Suddenly, each one grabbed onto a poodle, while Dad clung to a boogie board. The girls were exhausted and frightened. With their heads barely above water, the poodles struggled to stay afloat. The poodles were tiring quickly, frantically trying to keep everyone safe.

Poodles are known for their water skills and intelligence. The word "poodle" comes from the German "pudeln" which means "to splash in the water." The Germans call the breed "pudel" which means water dog. The French call it "caniche" which means "duck dog." You can tell from the German and French names for poodles that they are good swimmers. They are famous for their retrieving capabilities in water. Yet, even with all of their skills, the two poodles were exhausted keeping themselves and the children from drowning.

Ellen and Bobby were cruising on their small Jet Ski boat, a *Sea Doo* made to skim the surface of the water. They were enjoying the fading sun when suddenly Ellen heard a faint sound in the distance. She strained to figure out where it was coming from, not exactly sure what she was hearing. Finally, Ellen realized what the sounds meant -- a cry for help! Bobby slowed the boat, and the cries grew louder. In the distance, they saw a man waving to them as he clung precariously to a boogie board. He screamed to Ellen and

Portrait of a poodle
by Kara Dempsey

Bobby, pleading with them to find his two girls and the poodles. The man looked like he was able to hold on longer, so Ellen and Bobby searched for the kids.

Seventy-five yards away, the couple found two young girls, their heads barely above the water, grasping two poodles. The dogs and kids

 *all* looked very scared and tired. The dogs were fighting a losing battle against the current, and could hardly stay afloat. Ellen and Bobby drove their boat as close as possible, then pulled the girls to safety. There was not much room in the small boat, but Ellen was able to reassure the girls that they were safe. The girls were terrified that something would happen to their father, and two very brave dogs. Bobby started up the boat, shifted into gear, and raced across the water. The father was still hanging onto the boogie board. Quickly, they pulled him onboard. The father could not stop thanking them, saying over and over again, "God bless you. I will pray for you; thank you so much." He cried tears of joy. There was no more room for the dogs, so Ellen and Bobby brought the family to their boat and then rushed back to save the dogs. Ellen recalls what happened next.

The poor dogs were so tired and scared!
They were wet, heavy, and big, so it
was difficult to lift them onto the boat.
We just kept talking quietly to them. It's
strange to try to comfort dogs that you
don't know.

Sketch
by Samantha Hollander

Everyone was saved. Ellen considered the irony of how things worked out.

If we had done one thing differently, we
might not have been there at the right time
and place to save them. We could have read
about them in the newspaper the next day . . .

It was an emotional experience for everyone. With all of the tension, they forgot to exchange phone numbers. They never saw each other again. Even though they probably will never meet again, both the dogs and the people will never forget each other.

Poodle Points

Poodles are one of the oldest breeds known to humankind. No one knows the exact time the breed emerged, but carvings of poodle-like dogs have been

JOURNÉE DE PARIS
AU PROFIT DES
ŒUVRES DE GUERRE
DE L'HÔTEL DE VILLE
14 JUILLET 1917

World War I "poodle" poster, 1917

found as far back in Roman tombs and Greek and Roman coins. They were originally used as hunting and sporting dogs, known for their excellent swimming abilities. What is today known as the "poodle cut" was actually a clipping designed for added mobility, reduced chances of getting snagged, and warmth when in cold waters. The ribbon on a poodle's head was used to identify a dog when working in the water.

The poodle's intelligence and personality made it a perfect choice for traveling performers and gypsies. They trained their poodles to to do all kinds of tricks and routines, often dressed in costumes, and demonstrating amazing feats of balance and agility. Of course, it didn't take long before "fashionable ladies" were clipping, dying, and styling their poodles in an endless array of fashion statements, making "poodle" design a popular art. More recently, poodles have become the breed of choice for a whole new line of "designer mutts" that cross poodles with established purebreds. Some of these breeds include labradoodles, cockapoos, schnoodles, goldendoodles, maltipoos, and yorkipoos. These "doodle" dogs are known for their intelligence, temperament, and hypoallergenic coats.

Coco, the labradoodle sister of Gizmo

Today, poodles come in all colors and sizes. The oldest breed size is the standard, weighing 40-60 pounds, miniatures weigh 15-35 pounds, and toys tip the scales at less than 12 pounds. The newest additions, tiny toys and teacups, weigh 4-6 pounds, and 2-4 pounds respectively.

RUTLAND MANOR

written by:

| Yael | Melissa | Kara | Claire | Teddy |

I still remember Gizmo very well. He was a gorgeous puppy, the biggest in his litter, and a real cuddle bunny with a glorious rich chocolate-colored coat -- Beverley Manners

Beverley owns Rutland Manor Breeding and Research Center, where Gizmo was born. It's actually a farm, located in Darnum, Victoria, in Australia. In addition to labradoodles, there is a flock of Wiltshire horned sheep who Beverley describes as "moving from one dog park to the other on a rotational basis, keeping the grass mowed like a lawn." There are also seventy cows and calves, and quarter horses bred to be trained and shown. Most importantly, of course, are the labradoodles.

The Rutland Manor labradoodles are unique, unlike any other dog in

the world. They have thrived under Beverley's loving care.

Rutland Manor began as a dream back in 1989. Beverley had worked with animals all her life, as a dog trainer, dog show judge, managing a large chain of boarding kennels, and running her own grooming salon. The Royal Guide Dog Association in Melbourne had started breeding labradoodles -- a cross between a Labrador retriever and a poodle. "Everyone who saw one," Beverley adds, "wanted one." Guide dogs, however, are not for the public. Beverley saw a real need to develop the special qualities of these dogs.

Beverley spent a lot of time experimenting with the dogs from 1989 to 1997. She wanted a smart, friendly, non-aggressive dog with a hypoallergenic coat. In 1997, she found the right mix, registered her breed, and the research facility. She also went on the internet. Beverley called it "Rutland Manor." She researched the history of her full name, Beverley Frances Rutland-Manners.

Illustration by Claire Tucci

I discovered that the people called Manners originally lived in manors. The last German shepherd I had was called Rutland . . . it seemed like the natural name, and also in remembrance of my beloved Rutland who was my dearest friend and protector for many years.

Combining the names, she came up with Rutland Manor, a truly amazing place.

Several hundred puppies are born each year at Rutland Manor and in the three adjacent homes of guardian families. The puppies are bred with care and attention; the mothers "always have a loving mama or papa holding their paw when their babies are born." Each puppy has its own unique qualities and personality. When they're old enough, the puppies go to the main property to socialize, frolic in the stimulating labradoodle "Adventure Playground," and race through a "big five acre paddock with

Gizmo

mowed grass and shady trees." The indoor rooms have music, television, and cartoon characters painted on the walls. The system is designed to help puppies develop social and problem solving skills. Most important of all, the puppies are cuddled and loved by the staff. Beverley declares:

> *To work at Rutland Manor is to understand that the dogs ALWAYS come first.*

These special dogs are always matched to their owners. The staff gets to know the people who are buying a puppy so they can assure a great fit with family dynamics. It took years for Beverley to perfect the process. They use an application form, e-mails, and telephone calls to make character assessments. Gizmo is a great example.

> *He was an inquisitive puppy, always wanting to know what was going on and wanting to be part of it. He could never get enough of cuddling! He and Dr. Fink have turned out to be the perfect fit!*

There are three types of labradoodles: standard, medium, and miniature. Gizmo is a standard, and weighs about 85 pounds, or the size of a very large standard poodle. A medium labradoodle is the size of a small Labrador retriever. Gizmo's "little sister" Coco, is a miniature and weighs about 30 pounds. Rutland Manor's puppies are sent all over Australia, and to New Zealand, Tasmania, Singapore, Hong Kong, Hawaii, Norway, Japan, Switzerland, Holland, Canada, and throughout the United States. Gizmo and Coco live in New York, over 10,000 miles away from Rutland Manor.

The puppies do very well when traveling long distances because Rutland Manor desensitizes them for the trip. The puppies spend weeks

Coco
by Kara Dempsey

Adventure playground
by Claire Tucci

getting used to their travel crates while listening to television and airplane sounds. They arrive happy and healthy at their new homes.

Many celebrity dogs have come from Rutland Manor. Famous movie, radio, and television stars own labradoodles. Two Rutland Manor labradoodles starred in the stage production of *Annie* and another has a role in a Hawaiian TV show. Some sail on ocean cruises with their owners, some belong to High Court Judges and politicians. Many are trained service dogs that help disabled people around the world. Of course, there's Gizmo, the subject of many books, and Coco, with her first book, *Gizmo Gets A Wish*.

All the labradoodles at Rutland Manor are special in their own way. Perhaps this all emerges from Beverley's love of animals, deep concern for all the puppies and their future families, and her general love of life. One puppy's family says it best:

We've had several dogs in our lifetime, but never one like our labradoodle. She doesn't look "at" us, but seems to be looking right into our very souls.

Beverley loves her work, and the people and animals that fill her life. Beverley explains:

My favorite thing to do is to get into a gator (a motorized farm vehicle), take a few labradoodles with me, and go speeding across the paddocks with all the dogs running free around me. They race and gallop and are so beautiful to watch that my heart lifts and lurches just looking at them.

Beverley's Rutland Manor Album

THREE DOG BAKERY

written by:

Santino

Nicholas

Samantha

Christopher

"Dogs are not our whole lives," Roger Caras, the past president of the ASPCA (American Society for Prevention of Cruelty to Animals) once said, "but they make our lives whole."

Nowhere is this more true than with Dan Dye and Mark Beckloff, founders of the incredible Three Dog Bakery. It all began with Gracie.

Gracie

In 1988 Dan rescued a beautiful great Dane puppy whom he named Gracie. Gracie was an albino with white fur and gorgeous blue eyes who was born deaf, and blind in one eye. Dan recalls,

As dogs often do, Gracie came into my life at a time when I needed her the most. My life felt out of balance . . . I felt lost and confused. My job wasn't going anywhere . . . I needed help! I thought of Gracie as an angel, sent especially to me.

Suddenly, at six months old, Gracie stopped eating. Soon the great Dane looked very skinny and unhealthy. Dan recalls those difficult days.

Portrait of Gracie
by Chris Nazario

It takes a lot of nutrition to support a great Dane puppy, yet she had no interest in food. It was becoming scary -- a serious situation that even perplexed the veterinarian.

They tried to entice her with all different kinds of food, but nothing worked. Great Dane puppies grow quickly, sometimes as much as a pound a day. Gracie was looking dangerously "skeletal."

Desperate for a solution, the vet suggested that Dan and Mark start cooking for her.

It was a laugh, since we could barely keep ourselves fed let alone cook for our dog!

The first thing they made for Gracie was a vegetable and beef biscuit, freshly baked with whole grains, carrots, spinach, garlic, and a savory home-made beef broth.

It was wonderful . . .Gracie loved them and began to start cautiously eating again. That was the initial seed that, once planted, grew into our first Three Dog Bakery.

Three Dog Bakery opened in Kansas City, Missouri in 1989. The three dogs that were behind the creation of the bakery were Sarah Jean, an 88 pound black Lab mix, Dottie, a very spotted Dalmatian, and Gracie. At that point, Gracie, who was eating very well, weighed 140 pounds. Dan and Mark experimented on different recipes, using the three dogs to taste-test the results. Then the neighbors' dogs got a taste of the new creations. It was obvious that Dan and Mark had a real hit on their hands.

Today there are 31 Three Dog Bakeries, with 15 new stores scheduled to open. There are also five bakeries in Japan, two in South Korea, and two in Canada. Their products are sold in

Sarah, Gracie, and Dotti

107

Dottie

stores throughout the U.S., and in a booming mail order business. Three Dog Bakery maintains a nutritional, high quality, fresh product that uses only all-natural *human quality* ingredients. Dan explains how Three Dog is different.

Typically, dog food and treats have been a nasty, dirty business using only nasty, dirty ingredients. Three Dog Bakery is definitely breaking that mold!

Sadly, Gracie, Sarah Jean, and Dottie passed away at ripe old ages. "We still love and miss them terribly," says Dan. Now, the second generation of Three Dog Bakery pets goes to work with them everyday. Claire, a deaf great Dane, Dottie II, a Dalmatian/beagle mix, Biscuit, a small black Lab mix, and Lu, a pit bull puppy are all rescues.

We believe it is very important to help dogs in shelters by adopting them or rescuing them from terrible circumstances. One thing is guaranteed: your dog will soon become a very important and loved member of your family.

Sarah

Dan and Mark didn't stop there. They created the Three Dog Bakery Gracie Foundation. This amazing organization helps dogs in need or in emergency situations. They donate money and products to different groups throughout the country. In 2001, $90,000 was donated to help the dogs in New York City animal shelters that were abandoned after the 9-11 attacks. The Gracie Foundation also donates to groups affected by hurricane disasters, forest fires, and other natural calamities.

Three Dog Bakery has been seen all over the world! Dan and Mark hosted a cooking show for animals on the food network. They have also been on *The Oprah Winfrey Show*, *The Today Show*, *Late Night With Conan O'Brien*, *CNN,* and *Fox News*. They have been in many newspapers and magazines, including *The New York Times*, *The Los*

Angeles Times, and the cover of *Forbes Magazine*. They have several books, including *Amazing Gracie* which tells the story of how Gracie inspired the Three Dog Bakery.

Dan and Mark's second generation of dogs still go to the bakery every working day, like Gracie, Sarah Jean, and Dottie once did.

The dogs greet customers, eat all of the profits, sniff the mailman, sleep and walk around basically looking cute and cuddly all day. They make sure that our quality control standards stay at extraordinarily high levels.

**The next generation:
Dan, Mark, Claire, Dottie, and Sarah**

Illustration by Samantha Hollander

Grab a Three Dog Bakery shopping basset and get some cool treats like:

Scotti Biscotti

Itty Bitty Bones

Lick 'n Crunch Sandwich Cookies

Snicker Poodles

Fresh-baked Drooly Dream Bars

Itty Bitty Scary Kitties

Beagle Bagels

Personalized Dino Bones

Peanut Woofers

We Pity the Kitties Alaskan Salmon Cat Treats

Three Dog Bakery Art Gallery

Chow time
by Santino Larios

A sketch of Sarah
by Jackie Williams

Three Dog storefront
by Nadia Hernandez

Tales From The Net

The numbers are shocking -- 6 to 8 million dogs and cats enter shelters *every year.* Nearly half of them are euthanized -- potentially wonderful pets who could not escape the dog catcher's net. The other half are lucky. They end up in no-kill shelters, foster homes, rescue groups, or local pounds where someone notices them. Their stories vary from being born in the wrong place and time, to abuse and neglect, or dropped off because someone got sick, allergic, or left them tied to a tree.

These *Tales From The Net* are just a few of the many heroic human and canine stories where dogs have been saved, only to bring great joy to their families. The stories were written and e-mailed to the student-authors. They offer a glimpse into a humane community of people determined to make sure that our dogs find the homes they deserve.

Lou is a beagle that was abandoned at a fireworks show. He loves everyone.

Harley and Jackie are two rescues who now live with Yvonne and Adam in Northport, New York. Harley was abandoned at a veterinarian's office, and Jackie was adopted from a shelter.

The Clavin Family with Chanel, a rescued puppy. Chanel, two and one-half months old, was born in Georgia. She was scheduled to be euthanized. The family adopted her just in time.

Malcom was rescued from an empty building in Brooklyn, New York. He now lives with a great family in Sound Beach.

Nossle (with spots) and Misty are two Dalmatian rescues. They were found starving, weak, and covered with sores. The Commissioner of Uniondale Fire Department and his family adopted both dogs.

From: Joanne Anderson
To: Gizmo's Friends
Subject: How I got into dog rescue

I got involved in rescue work because of a chance encounter. The year after my husband and I got our first Afghan hound, we followed another older Afghan sitting in the back of a police car. We adopted him (Alfie) from the pound, after learning he had broken bones from life in several abusive homes. The last owners were drug addicts. He lived the rest of his life with us. While at the shelter, I was shocked to see so many nice dogs. I called Irish Setter Rescue to tell them about a dog, and the lady responded, "what do you want me to do?" I realized that I had to help. So I volunteered with PAWS.

I began writing a weekly rescue column in the "Babylon Beacon" newspaper. I was also a volunteer with the League for Animal Protection SPCA (LAP). Our goal was to make the public aware of the invisible because municipal shelters are usually hidden in industrial spots. The column consisted (and still does) of an information or anecdotal article followed by shelter photos and a list of available dogs/cats at Babylon Town Shelter. Each Saturday I visit the shelter to take photos and to socialize and care for the dogs. I name the poster dogs and sometimes dress them up for holidays. LAP also convinced the Town to let us take the dogs to various locations to promote adoptions. We called it "bringing the mountain to Mohammed".   :-)

The current dogs in my life are both rescues. Charlotte is a two year old English toy/Cavalier spaniel mix who was part of an SPCA raid of 33 tiny dogs abandoned in a Lindenhurst, New York, house. I placed all the surviving dogs, and had a huge family reunion hula party at the shelter last summer. Halle is a one year year old Afghan hound (my fifth one) taken from a neglectful home. She is stripped down because she was so matted. My husband tells strangers that the girls are from the same litter.

From: Nancy and Evelyn
To: Gizmo's Friends
Subject: Rescue Sisters

Hi guys! I'm Nancy Allegretti, and along with my sister, Evelyn Gomez, we rescue and find homes for unwanted dogs. We have been doing this for years and are very proud that we have a one hundred percent success rate with our adoptions. We are very strict on who will adopt the dogs that come to us and expect the potential new owners to fill out a very lengthy questionnaire. Evelyn then checks all references and the homes and then gives them to me to make the final match. The pairing of the right dog and owner is essential to making the match a success. We do not take any money for our efforts and will foster dogs ourselves until the right home and family is found. This has gotten me into trouble, though, for I have kept four rescues myself, three goldens and one St. Bernard. Zoie is my seven year old, Murphy is four, Holly is almost two, and Kali, my St. Bernard, is almost one. All of the dogs play well and get along great, though it is never very quiet in our home

Nancy Allegretti relaxes at home with her dogs:
(starting from the left first row) Adeline, Holly,
(second row from the left) Murphy, Kali, and Zoie.
All of the dogs, with the exception of Adeline, are
rescues.

From: Karen Schleich
To: Gizmo's Friends
Subject: Finding Forever Homes

Do you know how a dog is rescued? The first place a rescued dog or puppy goes is the vet, who gives them a check up, heart worm test, and vaccines. Then it's off to the groomer, for a bath, haircut, nails clipped, ears cleaned, flea check, and flea protection. The next stop is to go into boarding or a foster home, where I know that they will be fed walked, given treats, and sometimes just spoiled! For some dogs this is the only family life they've ever had, and we help socialize them to people, especially children, and other animals. We also walk them around Petco, bring them in the car, and spend a few days in doggie day care. It helps them adjust so they'll be ready to go into their "forever homes." Sometimes, the animals are sick and need extra medical care. My rescues never leave me until they're spayed or neutered. When they are placed in their new home, they bring treats, dog bowls a new bed, new collar and a leash. I always keep in touch with my rescues to make sure they're happy.

Karen and Cassidy, a Bernese mountain/ shepherd mix who was turned into a shelter at 8 years old.

Bear is a Newfoundland/chow mix. He is 11 years old and was rescued from a junkyard. Bear has bone cancer and will live the rest of his life with Karen.

Ginger, a 3 year old husky mix, that was tied to a tree with no food, water, or shelter. Ginger now lives with a family that loves her.

Valentino was kept in a cage too small for him, and now he has trouble walking. He will stay with Karen until he is able to be adopted.

119

From: Maria Menichetti
To: Gizmo's Friends
Subject: One Woman's Work

I started to rescue animals when I was young. I loved animals and went to school to study animal care. I worked at animal hospitals, and now I own a grooming shop. When people realized how I felt about animals, phone calls started coming in. People wanted my help with animals. Sometimes I needed to call the police to get animals away from abusive owners. Other animals are abandoned, left roaming dangerous roadways.

My friends all feel passionately about keeping animals safe. Not only do we rescue dogs, but we have saved birds, cats, and even reptiles. Most times, we have happy endings. Once I found a lost, starving dog wandering the streets. I kept him in my care, until I located its owner--a little girl who had been searching for her missing pet. I cherish the letter that the little girl sent to thank me.

I always keep my eyes and ears open, and wish everyone would help animals. Some of the animals I rescue I think of as my babies. I have a Dalmatian that was starved and had sores all over. My bulldog was rescued from September 11th. My shepherd was released into the streets while my Lab mix was a puppy of pack dogs just left by itself. All of them become part of my family.

One day I saw a homeless man and his dog begging for food. I discovered that even though homeless people have lost homes and jobs, many could not bear to lose their dogs. I decided to help a group of them that live in makeshift huts by the parkway. I collect dog sweaters, towels, blankets, dog toys, and food to help them out. If the dogs have any health problems, I try to get them what's needed.

Maria at work in her Bellmore, New York grooming shop,
Prim & Proper.

Lady Liberty was rescued after the terrorist attacks on 9-11.

Maria's ongoing collection for homeless people's dogs

121

From: Pamela Setchell
To: Gizmo's Friends
Subject: Viewpoint Photography

Pam and Johnny Rotten

One day, I received an important call from my friend who is a vet for the Guide Dog Foundation. She asked if I could give a retirement home to a very special guide dog named Knight. I quickly agreed, and Knight came to live with me.

After all, former guide dogs are extremely intelligent and friendly and have perfect manners -- who wouldn't want a dog like that at home?

Giving a retired guide dog a loving home is my way to help reward these amazing animals for a lifetime of hard, important work. They deserve the best.

Johnny Rotten, the cat in the photo, was rescued from Bide-A-Wee. He was abandoned at three weeks old, moved in, and took over my house. He and Knight are best friends. Sometimes Johnny Rotten cleans Knight's ears. Often they can be found curled up and sleeping together. They are very special to one another.

Knight was trained as a guide dog for a 26 year-old man named Terry. Terry was very active, but had lost his sight in his mid- twenties due to diabetes.

For 8 ½ years, Knight guided Terry in and out of Manhattan to college. They traveled on trains, subways, and just about every form of transportation. Terry went on to get his Bachelors Degree, Masters Degree and is now finishing up his Doctorate. He attributes this success to his wonderful dog Knight.

Knight started to show signs of slowing down. Terry felt that Knight gave him back his life and the admirable thing to do for Knight, was to retire him. He felt he should just go be a dog and not work anymore. Terry wanted him to go swim and play with other dogs and have some fun. This was a very hard decision for Terry as it meant giving up his *best* friend.

Knight came to me, and for a little over a year he enjoyed romping, playing, and swimming. Then he was diagnosed with diabetes. He lost the ability to walk well and eventually lost his sight. How ironic that a dog that guided a man who lost his sight due to diabetes, lost his own sight due to diabetes.

Knight is now completely blind. He has learned his way around the house, and hangs out with Johnny Rotten. He remains a wonderful and very loving dog.

BetsyBee was a guide dog for a blind woman who lived in Israel. One day, when the woman and Betsy were outside, there was a huge blast. Betsy was terrified by the sound of the explosion. From that point on, Betsy was sound shy and could no longer work effectively as a guide dog. If a car backfired, she was terrified and could not concentrate on keeping her owner safe. BetsyBee was then sent back to the United States to the Guide Dog Foundation in Smithtown, New York. She did not requalify to work so she needed a good home for retirement.

She came to live with me, and loves to lay on the couch and be lazy. However . . . she is terrified of thunderstorms.

Dolly was a yellow lab who worked as a guide dog for a blind woman in Brooklyn, New York. The woman sang and performed on stage with Dolly at her side. For 11 years, Dolly went everywhere with the woman, joining her on many performance stages. As Dolly grew older, her arthritis kept her from continuing on as a guide. The woman loved Dolly and wanted to keep her, but Dolly developed medical problems that required a sighted person to treat. The woman was devastated, but this time it was Dolly that needed the help. When she was 13 years old, Dolly went into retirement at my house. Unfortunately, Dolly died about eight months after she came to live with me. She was a truly wonderful creature. She tried her hardest to work up until the end. She would follow me everywhere as if I were blind. Everyone who knew Dolly misses her.

From: John Peel
To: Gizmo's Friends
Subject: Yule

My wife and I spent four years rescuing miniature pinschers in the New York area. This meant collecting dogs from homes and shelters, checking out their personalities and then screening people to find just the right homes for them. It's hard work, but there's nothing quite like seeing the perfect family adopting the best dog in the world! Some of the dogs, however, have stayed with us -- like Yule. One Christmas, we were called to the New York City shelter, where a min pin was about to be put to sleep because he was so aggressive. Min pins don't do well in shelters, they're small dogs and when they're scared they can get very nasty. But with a little love, they often come around quickly. Yule was terrified, and had two huge men backed into a corner, snarling at them when we first met him! But when we got him home, he licked us gratefully. We found he'd been tortured, and his legs were scarred and burned from being tied with wire. He needed a lot of help, so we kept him -- and have one of the best dogs in the world.

John Peel with Yule. Yule's legs are
scarred from wire burns. He had been
badly abused before John rescued him.

Dog Heroes of the Past

Dogs have lived near human beings for many thousands of years. Most people agree that today's dog is primarily descended from the wild gray wolf. Scientists have estimated that humans and dogs share a 14,000 year old relationship. No one knows exactly when the first dog was domesticated. However, canine bones have been found in many ancient archeological sites around the world. Theoretically, there are as many dog heroes in history as there are human heroes.

Our history books don't pay much attention to canine heroes. Dogs don't ask for places in timelines and museums. They don't create dramatic technologies, make great music, or lead revolutions. They are faithful, endearing, protective, and incredibly loyal. Many dogs, like Seaman, Meriwether Lewis' dog, played important roles in history. Others plunged into war, like Chips, Wolf, and Wimpy, never considering their own safety. The most important thing to these heroes was their human comrades.

We can learn so much from these heroes of the past. If we adopted their qualities, we would become better people, "heroes" in our daily lives. If we embraced the sense of responsibility, courage, and loyalty of these canine heroes, our planet would be a much finer place to inhabit!

Helen Keller and her dog, 1904
Library of Congress, Reproduction # LC-USZ62-78982

Poster, 1902
Library of Congress
Reproduction #LC-USZC4-12528

Poster, 1899
Library of Congress

Chris, one of the dogs in Robert Falcon Scott's exploration of Antarctica, 1910-1912
Library of Congress, Reproduction # LC-USZ62-101001

BALTO *written by:*

Stephanie

Gabriella

Christian

Kaylee

Life can change quickly and without warning. Balto, a half-wolf, half-Malamute sled dog went from a loser to a hero many times during his 11 years of life.

At first, no one was impressed with Balto. He was half-wolf so people didn't trust him. No one even thought he was a great sled dog until January, 1925, when a deadly diphtheria epidemic hit Nome, Alaska. Diphtheria is a disease that attacks the nose, throat, and mouth. Dr. Curtis Welch, the only physician in town, saw that children were sick and dying. He sent out an urgent plea for diphtheria medication.

Anchorage, almost 1000 miles south of Nome, had a lot of diphtheria medication. However, it was the middle of winter in Alaska. The airplane that normally flew in emergencies wasn't available. The second choice, a train, was snowbound. It was decided that the quickest way to transport the medication was with dog sled teams. A relay was organized of 20 mushers to hand off the medication. They faced icy cold and raging winds along the trail.

The first sled team left and after 52 miles handed off the medication. The second team took over. News of the dramatic race to save Nome's children spread around the world. People were mesmerized by the struggle in the far North.

Portrait of Balto
by Gabriella Long

Gunner Kaassen was in charge of the next-to-the-last relay team, with Balto as his lead dog. Their job was to pass the medication along to the final team, who would carry it into Nome.

Suddenly, a blizzard hit. Temperatures plummeted to minus 60 degrees Fahrenheit. Winds roared at 70 miles per hour. Kaassen was snowblinded, unable to see the difference between the snow-filled sky and white ground. He couldn't find the last relay team to hand off the medication. They were in real trouble, until Balto took over. Using instinct, courage, and determination, Balto led them through the fierce cold, blinding snow, and unrelenting ice. Kaassen could do nothing but hope that Balto was on the right trail.

On February 2, six days after the relay began, Balto led Kaassen and his team down the streets of Nome. The children were saved! People around the world celebrated the canine hero. Balto's story was told in newspapers; he was invited to make personal appearances, and he received medals and accolades. Balto was everyone's beloved hero.

Quickly, Balto became old news. People forgot about his heroism, newspapers didn't write about him, and no one gave him any more medals. Balto and his team were sold to a crude Vaudeville promoter. He made Balto and the dogs into a sideshow, the attraction of "dime-a-look" gawkers. In 1927, a Cleveland businessman accidentally discovered Balto and the remaining dog team. They were poorly kept and in bad health. Horrified, he turned to the people and pleaded for help.

People rushed to donate money to help Balto and the dogs. Children collected pennies in buckets; factory workers passed the hat around. Stores, visitors, and residents made generous donations. In two weeks they raised $2000 -- a fortune in 1927.

The money was used to purchase the dogs and bring them to the Cleveland Zoo. They spent the rest of their lives in a comfortable environment, with constant visitors. Balto died six years later. His body was preserved and put on display at the Cleveland Museum of Natural History. A bronze statue of Balto was erected in Central Park, New York City, and a movie and animated film were made about his life.

Perhaps Balto's greatest legacy is the race that memorializes him. In 1973, the first Iditarod Race was launched. Today, the over 1000 mile dog sled race, running from Anchorage to Nome, Alaska, is broadcast around the world. The race is held every year, a fitting tribute to a hero who continues to teach us about courage and determination.

Meet The Iditarod

Each year everyone in Alaska gets involved in what is known as the "The Last Great Race." It's an event that doesn't compare to any other competition on earth. The race runs over 1150 miles, through the roughest, most challenging country imaginable. There are jagged mountain ranges, rivers frozen solid, thick forests, desolate tundra, and windswept coastline. Competitors -- mushers and their dog teams -- face bitter arctic cold, blinding blizzards, and winds that blow at ferocious speeds. Often, there is a complete loss of visibility, long hours of darkness, and mind-numbing climbs.

It is perhaps the greatest continuing demonstration of human and canine bond in the history of both species.

Originally, the Iditarod Trail was used by native hunters, Russian explorers, fur traders, and gold prospectors. It was named for an Athabascan Indian village near the site of an early 1910 gold rush town

Dog sled arriving From Iditarod, 1912
Library of Congress, Reproduction #LC-USZ62-131749

in the Iditarod mining district. The U.S. Army surveyed the trail in 1908 and dubbed it the "Seward to Nome Mail Trail," but everyone continued to call it the Iditarod. It was a major Alaskan pathway heavily used until 1924, when the airplane replaced dog sleds.

The story of Balto and the race to get the medication to the children of Nome came at the end of the sled dog era. It was 40 years later when dog sledding returned to its glory. In the 1960's, a musher named Joe Reddington, Father of the Iditarod, introduced the new dog sled race. The first run went only 9 miles along the Iditarod trail. It quickly expanded, and by 1973, the route ran from Anchorage to Nome.

Today, the Iditarod is followed around the world. Mushers and their dogs are heroes, and their accomplishments are legendary.

Street scene, Anchorage ca. 1900-1930
Library of Congress, Lot 11453-1 no. 217

Nome, 1916
Library of Congress, Lot 11453-1 No. 344

Facts About The Iditarod Race

*The first race was won by Dick Wilmarth in 20 days, 49 minutes, 41 seconds in 1967.

*The last finisher receives a Red Lantern. The longest time for a Red Lantern was in 1973: John Schulz, in 32 days, 15 hours, 9 minutes, 1 second.

*The fastest finish was by Martin Buser, 2002, in 8 days, 22 hours, 46 minutes, 2 seconds.

*The first woman finisher was Libby Riddles in 1985.

*The youngest musher was 18-year old Ellie Claus.

*The oldest musher was 88-year old Norman Vaughn.

*The most wins was by Rick Swenson (5).

*The most wins by a woman was by Susan Butcher (4).

*The closest race was in 1978 when Dick Macky beat Rick Swenson by 1 second, after 2 weeks on the trail.

*Since 1983, the race has started in downtown Anchorage.

*Required race equipment includes arctic parka, heavy sleeping bag, ax, snowshoes, musher food, dog food, dog booties to protect paws against cutting ice and hard packed snow injuries.

133

BARRY *written by:*

Nicole   **Ryan**   **Joanna**   **Amanda**

Imagine a shelter that sits 8000 feet high, nestled in glacial slopes and walls of snow. The shelter or hospice protected weary people traveling the Great St. Bernard Pass. It was built in the Swiss Alps by Augustinian Monks during the 11th century. The monks were dedicated to a labor of aid and mercy for tradesmen, artisans, couriers, beggars, emperors, popes, pilgrims, and soldiers who passed on their way between Italy and Northern Europe. These travelers desperately needed help, especially during the frozen winter months. The monks even helped Napoleon's soldiers who passed through during the winter of 1800.

In the mid 17th century, the monks began to use a unique breed of dog to protect, rescue, and guide struggling mountain travelers. The dogs had an excellent sense of smell, were gentle, playful, and could rescue people caught in the deep snow, often buried by avalanches. Large, powerful, with enormous stamina for cold temperatures, and weighing up to 200 hundred pounds, the dogs were both companions and heroic workers. The breed was named St. Bernard, for the pass they patrolled.

Kali, a St. Bernard puppy from the Allegretti Family.

Barry was the most famous St. Bernard at the hospice. He lived with the monks from 1800-1812. Barry could do amazing things -- sense a storm was coming, detect an avalanche before it happened, find a person in up to 15 feet of snow, know when to bark and when to play, and how to make people feel comfortable and safe around him. Barry was able to negotiate the most dangerous

St. Bernard Hospice ca. 1890-1900
Library of Congress, Reproduction #LC-DIG-ppmsc-07892

whiteout conditions where humans can't tell the difference between the snow on the ground and snow in the air. Many people got lost and died in whiteouts unless Barry or the other St. Bernards were there to lead them to safety.

Barry saved 40 lives in this demanding environment. He didn't care if they were rich or poor, young or old, beggars or Napoleon's soldiers. As a rescue dog, Barry would track people in the snow, whether buried or lost, and lead them back to safety. Stories of Barry's famous rescues were passed around the world. One popular legend told about the day Barry and Brother Luigi went for a winter walk. Suddenly, there was an avalanche. Brother Luigi rushed back to the hospice, but Barry refused to follow. Instead, he tracked a little boy, licked him until he woke up, pulled the child from an icy ledge, and let the boy ride his back to safety. While the story is exaggerated, there is a good chance it is based on some truth! In 1822, a painting was made of Barry's famous rescue.

Barry died the same way he lived -- attempting to save a human life from the ravages of ice and snow. His body was brought to the Berne Museum of Natural History and preserved. Almost 200 years after his death, Barry still stands at the entrance to the museum. Perhaps his greatest legacy is that in every litter of St. Bernards born at the hospice, the most beautiful puppy is named "Barry" in his honor.

Sadly, today's helicopters and heat-sensors have taken over the job of the St. Bernards. In 2004, the now-tiny hospice announced they were giving up their remaining St. Bernards. Brother Frederick, a monk at the hospice, explained that the dogs "need a lot of time and energy." The monks could no longer maintain the 300 year old tradition.

Miraculously, almost a year later, *Reuters* ran a dramatic headline, *Ghost of Barry Bounds to the Rescue of St. Bernards*. Animal-loving philanthropists donated money to create "The Barry of the Great St. Bernard Foundation," dedicated to preserving the dogs, running a museum, and maintaining the heroic canine residents of St. Bernard Pass. Barry had successfully completed yet another rescue.

SEAMAN *written by:*

Brandon

Jimmy

C.J.

Allie

Not many people realize that the skills and courage of a huge shaggy black dog were instrumental to the success of Lewis and Clark's famous expedition. Seaman, a Newfoundland dog, along with a total of nearly four dozen humans, joined the legendary journey to explore the newly acquired Louisiana Purchase. Seaman was purchased by Meriwether Lewis for $20 in 1803, which is equivalent to more than $300 today.

Seaman is an unusual name for a dog unless you're a Newfoundland. Newfoundlands were standard crew on fishing boats in the Canadian maritime province that gave the breed its name. Big, sweet, and obedient, the breed is known for its amazing swimming ability. The dogs held many jobs, such as rescuing men who fell overboard, saving drowning victims, retrieving objects from the water, and hauling fishing nets out to sea. It was no surprise that Meriwether Lewis chose a Newfoundland to join his expedition.

Meriwether Lewis
Library of Congress
Reproduction #LC-USZ62-20214

Lewis kept a journal during the entire trip, detailing all their adventures, including those of his beloved dog. He wrote about how Seaman was a good hunter and guard dog. He was strong, with great character. Seaman lived up to all expectations. One of Lewis' earliest journal entries described how Seaman helped out:

The squirrel appears in great abundance on either side of the river. I made my dog take as many each day as I had occasion for, they wer fat and I thought them when fryed a pleasant food.

In another journal entry on November 16, 1803, Lewis carefully noted exactly what he was offered for his "prised" dog:

. . . a respectable looking Indian offered me three beverskins for my dog with which he appeared much pleased . . . I prised much for his docility and qualifications generally for my journey and of course there was no bargain.

Ziggy, a Newfoundland member of the Courtien family

Seaman helped the human explorers survive. Lewis wrote about how the dog sensed danger from wild animals and barked continuously to wake everyone. He warned them of predators like bears and bison, and almost died when a beaver bit him through the hind leg and ripped open his artery. Lewis wrote mournfully of one incident:

It was with great difficulty that I could stop the blood. I fear it will yet prove fatal to him.

Seaman survived, completing the 8000 miles covered by the expedition in almost two and one-half years. Near the end of their journey, the explorers showed their love for the dog by naming a "large creek 20 yds. wide" in his honor: Seaman's Creek.

No one knows exactly what happened to Seaman after the expedition. Lewis didn't mention him again in his journal. In September, 1806, the expedition made a

triumphant return to St. Louis, and the humans were immediately declared national heroes. Was Seaman with them?

Thomas Alden, a well-respected historian in the early 1800's, wrote a book in 1814. He told the following, heartbreaking story about Lewis and Seaman. Meriwether Lewis died in 1809, at age 35. No one knows why, although many believed he was murdered. It still remains a mystery. Alden wrote that Seaman was with Lewis when he died, and later refused to leave Lewis' grave. The incredibly loyal dog eventually starved to death next to his beloved owner's tomb.

Although we are not sure what happened, it is definite that Seaman was a brave and loyal explorer who left his big, shaggy paw print in American history.

Portrait of Seaman
by C.J. DiMaggio

Lewis & Clark holding council with the Indians
Library of Congress, Reproduction #LC-USZ62-17372

Expedition Trivia

*Lewis and Clark spent $2,324 for gear.

*Sacagawea was the only woman on the expedition. She had been kidnapped from her native Shoshone tribe at 12 years old, and later sold to French-Canadian fur trader, Toussaint Charbonneau. She became a valuable interpreter for Lewis and Clark, and the teenage mother to Jean Baptiste, whom Clark nicknamed "Pomp."

*To prepare for the expedition, Meriwether Lewis studied natural sciences, astronomical navigation, field medicine, and a list of questions to ask American Indians about their daily lives.

*The expedition was commissioned by President Thomas Jefferson and called the "Corps of Discovery."

*During the expedition there were disciplinary floggings, two desertions, and one dishonorable discharge for mutiny.

*There was only one death during the entire expedition -- an amazing accomplishment at the time. Sgt. Charles Floyd died of what is suspected to have been a ruptured appendix.

*Meriwether Lewis was 28 years old when he began the expedition, William Clark, was 32 years old.

*Lewis and Clark both kept detailed journals and maps.

*Today, the expedition has become big business. There are websites, online "tours," puzzles, games, books, videos, and commemorative products.

*Tour companies arrange trips that follow the footsteps of the expedition!

War Dogs

**Charlie Cargo, keynote speaker at the
annual War Dog Memorial Service
in Hartsdale Pet Cemetery.**

Throughout history when people go to war, so do dogs. Dogs have been in active service at the sides of soldiers from the days of the Egyptians, Greeks, and Persians to the more recent wars in Vietnam and Iraq. By showing bravery under fire, saving lives (often by sacrificing their own), and bringing comfort to the injured, dogs have proven themselves as heroes.

While war dogs have accompanied famous conquerors such as Atilla the Hun and Napoleon, their role has changed in modern times. War dogs are more likely to be used as *protectors* rather than attackers. They're out in the field to save lives, not take them. Many work as sentries or patrols to alarm troops to impending danger. Others lead their handlers to hidden weapons, explosives, and drugs. Dogs are even being used to detect terrorists and suicide bombers.

War dog stories are as varied and dramatic as the tales told by soldiers. They are about unspoken courage, loyalty, and a fierce determination to protect their comrades-in-arms. Unfortunately, the dogs have not always received the honors they deserve, best demonstrated by the military at the end of the Vietnam war. Today that is changing with the help of people like Charlie Cargo, who reveal the spirit of these true military heroes.

1917 World War I poster
Library of Congress,
Reproduction #LC-USZC4-9555

War Dog Facts by Charlie Cargo

*Thirty thousand dogs have served America in the past 50 years. Civilian dogs were volunteered by their families for service in World War II, and they were considered personnel by the Defense Department. Some of them were promoted to outrank their handlers. At war's end, these dogs received Honorable Discharges and were returned to civilian life.

*During the Korean War, a study concluded that war dogs cut casualties by more than 65 percent wherever they worked on the front line. One scout dog named York completed 148 combat patrols without a single loss of life. From this time forward, war dogs would be classified as "equipment," and stripped of their ranks and honorary medals.

*Three thousand scout and sentry dogs went to Vietnam to protect our troops, and in the course of the war, they saved over 10,000 lives. Fewer than 200 dogs ever saw American soil again. Because they were now considered "equipment," they either were euthanized in the country (under orders from our government), or they were handed over to the Army of the Republic of Vietnam, which slaughtered them for meat, bartered the hides for Viet Cong bounties, or let them perish from neglect.

*Today's war dogs are drafted for life. As long as they can work, they can live. When they become too old to serve, they get euthanized. Nobody goes home. Not yet . . . but perhaps some day it will be very different, only if we care enough to change the system

First commemorative war dog envelope
January 1, 2000
United States Postal Office

141

General Rufus Ingall's horse and dog,
1865
Library of Congress
Reproduction #LC-DIG-CWPB-02002

Lt. George Custer with dog, 1862
Library of Congress
Reproduction #LC-DIG-CWPB-01553

Group of Co. A
8th New York State Militia
1861
Library of Congress
Reproduction #LUSZC4-0785

Monument for Sarge, World War II hero dog
Bide-A-Wee Memorial Park

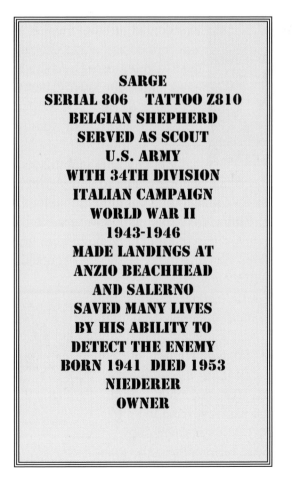

SARGE
SERIAL 806   TATTOO Z810
BELGIAN SHEPHERD
SERVED AS SCOUT
U.S. ARMY
WITH 34TH DIVISION
ITALIAN CAMPAIGN
WORLD WAR II
1943-1946
MADE LANDINGS AT
ANZIO BEACHHEAD
AND SALERNO
SAVED MANY LIVES
BY HIS ABILITY TO
DETECT THE ENEMY
BORN 1941 DIED 1953
NIEDERER
OWNER

CHIPS *written by:*

Stephanie

Stephen

Danny

Michael

Chips, 1943

The most famous World War II dog, Chips, was denied military medals of honor. Chips was trained and shipped overseas to serve with the Third Infantry Division. He quickly earned a reputation for loyalty, bravery, and fearlessness. He faced danger without hesitation, and fought side-by-side with the soldiers he loved.

World War II mobilized a patriotic public willing to do anything to help American soldiers in combat. A new group called "Dogs for Defense" joined forces with the American Kennel Club (AKC) asking people around the country to donate quality dogs to the war effort. The dogs were trained to help save soldiers' lives. Chips was one of the first dogs accepted into the program.

Born in Pleasantville, New York, Chips was the pup of a collie-shepherd father and northern sled dog mother, donated by Edward J. Wren.

More than 19,000 dogs were donated between 1942 and 1945. In the beginning, 30 different breeds were accepted. Eventually, the list was restricted to German shepherds, Belgian sheep dogs, doberman pinschers, farm collies, and giant

Portrait
by Stephanie Massucci

schnauzers. Fifty-five percent of the donated dogs went on for training in the Quartermaster Corps.

Chips' first assignment was in General Patton's fierce assault in North Africa. He was then shipped out to Sicily. Chips and his unit made their way ashore, headed towards an empty machine gun nest. Unlike soldiers who read maps and carry guns, Chips only had his instincts. As the unit neared the empty nest, they decided to rest. Chips couldn't sit still. He sensed danger and broke a cardinal rule -- Chips ran away from his handler. At that moment, no one realized that Chips had decided to break the rule so he could save his men! Suddenly, shots rang out. Chips was hit, but the heroic dog ignored the pain. He kept on running, and threw himself into the machine gun nest. The firing stopped. There was dead silence. No one saw or heard Chips. Slowly, the soldiers edged toward the nest. They looked inside and found Chips gripping the throat of the enemy gunner while holding five terrified men at bay, their hands in the air and their guns on the ground.

Lieutenant Lucian Truscott recommended Chips for the Silver Star and Purple Heart, saying that the dog demonstrated:

. . . courageous action and prevented injury and death to his men.

Chips was denied the award. The Army said he disobeyed his handler by breaking away, and medals were for men, not dogs.

It didn't affect Chips' loyalty and dedication. He went on to serve in Italy, France, and Germany. He was also chosen to be the sentry dog for the Casablanca Conference between President Franklin Delano Roosevelt and Prime Minister Winston Churchill, in 1943.

Chips was sent home in 1945. He died seven months later from complications related to his war injuries. He was only six years old. Years later, in 1993, Disney produced a movie called *Chips, The War Dog.* Chips certainly showed us a very special brand of heroism.

Portrait of Chips,
by Michael Iacono

Wimpy's Story

The house stood on open land, surrounded by farms in Rosedale, New York. It had been built by Peter Bendzlowicz for his wife and young children. The family owned Wimpy, an extraordinary two-year old German shepherd who loved to eat hamburgers. He was named after a comic book character from *Popeye*. Wimpy was Popeye's loyal friend -- the chubby guy always eating a hamburger.

Wimpy was a very special dog. One day, Wimpy was agitated and Peter couldn't calm the dog. Wimpy kept on moving back and forth, as if he wanted Peter to follow. Finally, Peter let Wimpy take the lead. It was bitter cold but the dog didn't care -- he led Peter down two blocks, straight to Rosedale Creek. Peter was shocked! Two kids had fallen into the creek and were stuck in the ice. They would have drowned or frozen to death if Wimpy hadn't come to the rescue.

Wimpy was the hit of the town! No one was prouder of the dog than five-year old Peter Jr. The two were inseparable.

In 1942 a call went out to the American public. World War II was raging, and the military needed civilians to donate brave, intelligent, dogs to help the soldiers. The Bendzlowicz family knew Wimpy was the kind of dog that would save lives. They looked at their beloved pet and felt that they would do anything to help the soldiers at war. With both sadness and pride, Wimpy was donated to the military.

On February 18, 1943 -- two weeks before Wimpy left for military assessment and training, the Bendzlowicz family took these photos.

Peter Jr. and Wimpy

Peter Jr. and Wimpy with
the family's 1935 Hudson

Peter Sr., Wimpy, and Peter Jr.

On March 3, 1943, Wimpy arrived at the Widener Estate in Elkins Park, Pennsylvania, for assessment by the *U.S. Coast Guard Dogs for Patrol.* The following letter was mailed to the Bendzlowicz family.

U. S. COAST GUARD DOGS FOR PATROL

WIDENER ESTATE, ELKINS PARK, PA.

Mr. Peter P. Bandzlowitz

147 - 29 259 Street,

Rosedale, L.I., N.Y.

YOUR DOG __Wimpy__ ARRIVED __March 3, 1943__
APPARENTLY IN __Good__ CONDITION.

IF, AFTER A THOROUGH TRIAL, THE DOG IS ACCEPTED, YOU WILL RECEIVE AN

OFFICIAL CERTIFICATE. IF, FOR ANY REASON, IT IS REJECTED, YOU WILL BE

NOTIFIED IMMEDIATELY.

THANK YOU FOR YOUR PATRIOTISM.

JOHN H. CREIGHTON
Lieutenant (j.g.) U.S.C.G.R.

Wimpy was assessed at Widener Estate and selected to be a patrol dog. He was trained to enter the war effort. The Bendzlowicz family received a service flag with a gold star to hang in their window. The flag told everyone that a member of their family was serving in the military. It was the flag that all military families hung in their windows when someone was fighting in the war. Wimpy's family was given the same respect as millions of military families across the country.

Wimpy's life changed dramatically. He would never again see the Bendzlowicz family or his beloved Peter Jr.

Dogs in the Coast Guard
U.S Coast Guard

U.S. Coast Dogs for Patrol was established in July, 1942. It had been eight months since the attack on Pearl Habor and the subsequent United States entry into World War II. Americans were frightened; many were convinced that it was only a matter of time until the war directly hit the continental United States. Clearly, the greatest vulnerability was on the coast, where shipping and enemy infiltration did not present a big risk to the enemy. On June 13, 1942, it seemed as if America's worst fears had come true.

During the foggy night, a U-202 boat (that was submerged at day and surfaced at night) anchored off the coast of Long Island, New York. Four Nazi agents came ashore in a rubber raft. They were led by George Dasch, an American. When they reached the beach, the Nazis changed from military fatigues to civilian clothing and buried their uniforms.

Twenty-one year old John Cullen, Seaman 2nd Class, was patrolling a six-mile area outside of Amagansett Station. Cullen heard voices

149

speaking in a language that sounded like German. He approached the group and Dasch said "We're fishermen from Southampton and ran aground here."

Cullen had no weapons or radio, so he raced back to the station to report the intruders. When morning came, the beach was searched. They found the uniforms, as well as explosives and incendiary devices. The FBI was notified and the manhunt was initiated.

Four nights later, another group of Nazis infiltrated the beach in Ponte Vedra, Florida. Both groups of Nazis were eventually arrested and tried. By July, the Navy announced that

Dog beach patrol, Parramore Beach
U.S. Coast Guard

> *. . . beaches and inlets of the Atlantic, Gulf, and Pacific Coast would be patrolled by the Coast Guard whenever and wherever possible.*

The patrolmen were armed with rifles, sidearms, and fire pistols. They used horses and dogs to help cover nearly 4000 miles of vulnerable coast.

The call went out to donate dogs. The Coast Guard alone received about 2000 dogs to help in the patrols.

Wimpy was accepted by the Coast Guard and trained for duty on the 300 acre Widener Estate. Wimpy was paired with a handler and assigned to foot patrol. Most of the patrols were at night, along the shore, in all kinds of weather. In some areas where "sand pounders" (dogs, people, and horses) couldn't pass, boats and motor patrols took over. Sometimes jeeps were used to cover rugged, isolated areas. Wimpy and his handler patrolled an area about one mile long. The horse patrols worked the coastal areas from New Jersey and southward. A 1997 article from *The Reservist* described the process:

> *. . . the sand pounders are gray, and the horses and dogs are long gone. Yet, for a brief, tense period of our nation's history these Coast Guardsmen guarded the very edges of American soil, linking two defensive strategies that put Coast Guardsmen on horseback and dogs by their sides.*

**Coast Guard Seaman
and dog on patrol**
U.S. Coast Guard

Two years after the Coast Guard Dogs for Patrol was founded, it appeared that the coastline was secured. There were no more enemy landings or incidents. The military decided to cut back on the patrols, and many of the animals were put into service in other locations.

The Bendzlowicz family received a letter from the military saying that Wimpy was being transferred. He was headed for Germany.

Several months later, the family received another letter. The military informed them, with much regret, that Wimpy had been killed in Germany. It was the same kind of letter sent to families who had lost loved ones in the war.

Peter Bendzlowicz, Jr. grew up and served in the Army Chemical Corps. He married, had three children, and became a commercial airline pilot. He built his own house, just like his father, in Wading River, New York -- not very far from where the Nazis had landed on Long Island.

In all those years, Peter never really forgot his beloved Wimpy.

One day, Peter's wife, Greta went shopping in town. She was headed for the meat store when she saw a stray puppy. Greta asked the storekeepers about the stray, but they had no information. They put out food so the homeless puppy wouldn't starve. Greta took the puppy home, not sure if Peter wanted a dog in the house.

Peter was shocked when he saw the puppy. It was as if Wimpy had come back to life -- with the same look,

Wimpy II

intelligence and playfulness of his childhood pet. Peter named the puppy, Wimpy II. In one of those strange coincidences of life, Wimpy had finally returned to the Bendzlowicz family.

RIN TIN TIN *written by:*

Rebecca

Andrew

Zack

Lauren

Rin Tin Tin is a lot more than one dog. He's a legacy that began with a puppy in a bombed-out, French dog kennel, and spanned the Atlantic

A Rin Tin Tin descendant

for 100 years (and still going). At one point, Rin Tin Tin received 10,000 fan letters each week, had his own phone number, and was considered a Hollywood star. Three generations of people have devoted their lives to preserving the pedigree of what is considered the most recognized German shepherd in history.

It all began during World War I, on September 15,1918, when Corporal Lee Duncan and his battalion went to check out a bombed out dog kennel in Lorraine, France. The only survivors were Betty, and her litter of five, ten-day old puppies. Duncan chose two puppies and named them after the puppets that French children gave to American soldiers for good luck: Rin Tin Tin and Nannette. They were the only puppies from Betty's litter that survived to adulthood. Duncan trained them to be war dogs. He was amazed by their ability to learn and work with people. When the war ended, Duncan decided to bring the dogs home with him to Los Angeles.

During the trip, Nannette got very sick and died. Fortunately, Rin Tin Tin remained healthy. Once home, Duncan attended dog shows with Rin Tin Tin. At one show, the German shepherd amazed everyone by jumping 13 ½ feet in the air! After the show, a man approached Duncan. His name was Darrell Zanuck, and he wanted to try out his revolutionary new camera that took moving pictures. Zanuck paid Duncan $350 for

Rin Tin Tin's performance.

Duncan saw a good deal and contacted every studio in Hollywood, offering his dog and a script. No one was interested. One day, he saw a crew trying to film a very uncooperative wolf. The crew was from a new studio on the verge of bankruptcy. Duncan convinced them to give Rin Tin Tin a chance. The dog gave an impeccable performance and the studio, Warner Brothers Pictures, made Rin Tin Tin a star.

Rin Tin Tin went on to make 26 films for Warner Brothers Pictures. As one of their leading "men," Rin Tin Tin was so famous that he was the only dog listed in the Los Angeles telephone directory. In 1932, at the age of 16, Rin Tin Tin died in the arms of Jean Harlow, one of Hollywood's most famous actresses.

Rin Tin Tin's legacy continued down the line. Rin Tin Tin II and Rin Tin Tin IV starred in one of the most popular canine shows ever, *The Adventures of Rin Tin Tin* (ABC, 1954-1959). Lee Duncan died in 1960, entrusting the legacy to Jannettia Brodsgarrd Propps at Bodyguard Kennel. Propps owned a son of Rin Tin Tin IV, named "Rinty." Her young granddaughter, Daphne Hereford, joined Propps in assuring that the legacy would continue. Hereford describes her role:

If you are at the helm of something as important as the
Rin Tin Tin legacy, then you are charged with a responsibility
to ensure that it remains the same as it was intended by its founders.

In 1957, Rin Rin Tin incorporated into several divisions including linebred descendants, fan and canine ambassador clubs, dog food, productions, museum, and teaching center. It established a unique foundation called ARFkids which is an acronym for **A R**inty **F**or Kids. The mission of ARFkids is :

To provide disabled and terminally ill children Service Dog
candidates that will be specifically trained to assist in the
improvement of the quality of life and accessibility of the child.

Thanks to women like Propps and Hereford, and the courage and loyalty of a puppy discovered in a bombed out kennel, the legacy continues to thrive.

Meet ARFkids -- a Rin Tin Tin legacy

ARFkids makes a difference.

They carefully choose puppies who come from the Rin Tin Tin bloodline, making sure they are mentally and physically healthy. These puppies will become highly trained service dogs to help children with many different disabilities.

The puppies are placed in the ARFkids In-Home Training Program. Families actively participate in the raising, training, and socialization of their service dogs, establishing a powerful connection right from the beginning. Professional trainers guide the families throughout the entire process.

Puppies accompany the families wherever they go, so the dogs get used to traffic, crowds, stores, football games, and community events. They also require extensive obedience, task, and specific skills training. It usually takes about two years to fully train a service dog.

The dogs help disabled children, six to 18 years old, gain flexibility and independence. The kids have many disabilities, from autism, traumatic brain injury, developmental disabilities, balance, walking, etc. Rhonda Barbieri, from the ARFkids Board of Directors, and mother of William, an ARFkid recipient says:

Portrait of Rin Tin Tin
by Lauren Amatulli

ARFkids has helped us along a road that will forever be remembered as an incredible journey!

Barbieri lives in Kansas City, Missouri, with her husband Michael, three children, and several other pets. She wrote the following story about her son William to illustrate how their lives were changed by ARFkids.

154

A Note from William's Mom

William and Sylverfox

William is what most people would regard as a pretty quirky little man. Actually he is only ten years old, but he says things that you might hear at a cocktail party attended by professors and faculty of a prestigious college. One of William's best friends is only four. Although there is a large age difference no one seems to notice. What they do notice is that his friend is a 90 pound German shepherd named Rin Tin Tin's Sylverfox.

Most people do ask, "Why do you have a dog? Why is he at the grocery store with you?" He doesn't just hear this question at the grocery store, but also at the theater, church, amusement parks, everywhere he goes. It is not an easy question to answer but William always answers, "Because I have seizures and have autism." That does not really answer the question, but it is the reason William and Sylverfox were introduced to one another. William was diagnosed before kindergarten with an autism spectrum disorder and later as having seizures.

What Sylverfox does for William is allow him to have some autonomy and independence, a chance to grow up and have a life similar to most of his classmates. How he does that can be partly attributed to his heroic forefathers. You see, he is the son of the current Rin Tin Tin, part of a long line of heroes dating back to the first Rin Tin Tin who was

rescued from a bombed out kennel in France during World War I.

The other part of his success is due to training -- time spent with William's mother and father, his sisters and whole family to prepare him to accompany William everywhere. It took a great deal of understanding on everyone's part and not just a little work and care.

The idea of training a service dog for children with autism was very new when this endeavor began. There was no one that formally did such a thing at the time, so it was all a great adventure in knowing what a dog could help William accomplish. What surfaced was an amazing line of tasks that could be done very quietly and without drawing undue attention to a child's disability.

When William walks around he has some spatial awareness difficulties. Roughly translated, it's as if he were walking down a staircase and thought there was one more step . . . but there was not, or that the steps were done, but they weren't. Everyone has had those moments, so it is easy to explain it that way. But William is never sure where his feet may fall on any steps, whether it's a stairway or level ground. That would be a most disconcerting feeling to be sure, but now he has a four footed, furry, walking handrail to give him a sense of the terrain.

Other concerns for William are becoming over-stimulated. Too many sounds and too many moving objects can jam up his thoughts. It's like opening too many windows in a computer program; he cannot process all of the information at once, and some people with autism try to do just that. They cannot block out background noise or lights and movement. Sylverfox helps William by offering a familiar focus, while de-escalating the overwhelming sensory input. His service dog will gently nudge him to signal he is starting to get stressed and should take a break. Sylverfox also alerts him to impending

seizures, which allows him time to seek appropriate places to rest or be safe.

There are many small things that Sylverfox has done to assist William since he has been in his life. Some are trivial to most people, but insignificant things like nudging William to move along in a line or to continue a task he has started, have made a very big difference to William and how he is perceived by others. William has even gone to Disney World with his family *and* Sylverfox. Sylverfox and the whole family met Mickey, rode on the rides (Sylverfox and William sat out the roller coasters), and took in some shows. There would have been no way to have a happy family trip to such an overwhelming place had William not had Sylverfox to help him. No little boy wants to be dependent on his mother for everything. It truly was the most magical place on earth, and it wasn't because of a mouse, it was all about the family and the dog.

The Gift From Captain Max von Stephanitz

In 1889 the Captain set out to standardize a breed of intelligent, wolf-like herding dogs. The dogs were agile, powerful, steady, and easy to train. Using his military discipline, he bred a dog based on "utility and intelligence" and founded the *Verein fur Deutsche Schaferhunde* or the German Shepherd Dog Club.

The Captain based the breed standard on mental stability and utility. They were designed to be working dogs.

Germany made good use of the new breed in World War I. They were used as Red Cross dogs, messenger dogs, supply carriers, tracking, and guard dogs. Back in the United States, everything German was being rejected. The American Kennel Club even changed the name of the breed to *shepherd dog.*

It took the end of World War I, and a German shepherd puppy from France to change public opinion. The puppy's name was Rin Tin Tin.

WOLF written by:

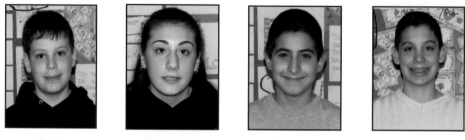

| Ben | Samantha | Frankie | Kevin |

Some superheros don't fly, wear a cape, or play music. They just have character, courage, and four legs.

Soldiers have used dogs for as long as war existed. In the middle ages, dogs wore armor and rushed into battle. Highly trained war dogs have been used on land, at sea, and even in the air. The war in Viet Nam was no exception, where approximately 4000 dogs saw action, saving at least 10,000 American lives. The dogs were used to detect enemies, bombs, and other weapons. They also guarded the camps. German shepherds were most common because they were loyal, smart, and learned fast. Wolf was one of them.

Charlie Cargo and Wolf in Viet Nam

Wolf was a highly trained scout dog who could locate enemy trip wires, traps, and troops up to 1000 yards away. He was a legend long before Charlie Cargo arrived in Viet Nam. Charlie was a draftee when he landed in Viet Nam in 1970. He was sent straight to the 48th Scout Dog Platoon in Chu Lai and assigned to Wolf. Wolf had to teach Charlie the ropes. Charlie describes his partner:

Wolf worked so hard to teach me what he was trained to do . . . he became my best friend, brother, teacher, and my lifesaving companion.

Over the 11 months they were partners, Wolf and Charlie safely led hundreds of soldiers through the jungles. One of the most famous stories was on a day when Wolf and Charlie were scouting a barren slope ahead of a battalion of soldiers. Suddenly Wolf stopped and sat down. Charlie couldn't see anything -- but he couldn't get his dog to move. Wolf just sat, not sniffing the air or listening to anything Charlie said. The soldiers behind them were getting frustrated, convinced that the dog was wasting their time. Annoyed, Charlie started to move past Wolf. Swiftly, the dog grabbed his hand and bit down hard, making blood trickle down his wrist. Charlie was shocked -- trained dogs never bit their handlers. Then he saw it. . .

A trip wire the thickness of a hair. Two feet in front of me.
My knees began to shake as the realization of just how close
I'd come to dying began to sink in -- and how I would have
taken Wolf with me.

When it was time for Charlie to leave Viet Nam, his family and friends begged the army to discharge Wolf and let him come home. They were denied. In desperation, Charlie requested to extend his tour of duty so he could remain with Wolf. That was denied, too. Charlie was ordered to bring Wolf back to the dog detachment center before he left. Sadly, Charlie slipped a muzzle on Wolf.

This dog . . . had nothing but love in his heart for his brothers-in-arms. I will never forget the confusion on his face when I walked away forever.

Charlie and Wolf never saw each other again.

When the Army withdrew from Viet Nam in 1973, the war dogs were classified as "surplus equipment" and left behind. Only a few made it back to the states. Wolf was one of them -- but the Army never notified

Wolf
by Kevin Archbold

Charlie that his beloved companion had survived. It took nearly 30 years for Charlie to learn the truth.

If you have ever had a pet, friend, or relative that you feel so close to, then you understand how much Wolf meant to Charlie Cargo. It's tragic that the Army never told Charlie that Wolf was stateside. They should have been united. Perhaps Charlie and Wolf will always be together in their hearts, both true American war heroes.

Charlie and Wolf safely led hundreds of troops through the jungles of Vietnam. They were a team both on and off-duty. "More than master and servant, more than brothers, we were of one heart and soul," he says today. When Charlie realized he was about to be separated from Wolf because he'd been promoted to Sergeant, he deliberately mouthed off to a superior so he would be busted back down to Sp/4, the equivalent of a Corporal. He was denied.

As his tour of duty drew to a close, Charlie's family telephoned dozens of military higher-ups, pleading for Wolf to be discharged so he too could come home. Their request was rejected.

Wolf's fate was a mystery for 30 years, but recently discovered documents indicate that he was one of the few "lucky" dogs to get stateside as the war wound down. In March 1972, he returned to Lackland Air Force Base in San Antonio, Texas and was diagnosed with testicular cancer. He was neutered and put back to work, until 1979, when he succumbed to lymphoma.

Charlie Cargo

Presidential Pups

A Presidential Pup is a very different kind of hero. They don't save people from fires, defend troops, or go on rescue missions. Their heroism comes from supporting some of the most important people in history.

Often, "man's best friend" in the White House is his only friend. When times got tough, these dogs stayed by their President's side, demonstrating loyalty, love, obedience, and companionship.

Most of these dogs lived in the White House. Many were more popular with their constituents than the Presidents they served. The dogs met world leaders, boosted Presidential popularity, and entertained wealthy, powerful dignitaries. They endeared themselves to millions of people, speaking a language that rises above politics.

Presidential Pups often reveal a different side of their owners. What kind of man has a special chair made so his dog can sit in cabinet meetings? What does it say when a man uses his dog to deflect negative public opinion? Who bonds with his dog when the whole country, including his wife and daughter, rejects him for bad behavior?

If everyone behaved more like the Presidential Pups, the world would have fewer problems. Our world would be safer, better, and perhaps there would be an end to war. We would be loyal friends to one another, kind neighbors, and happier people. People can learn so much from these amazing canines.

President Calvin Coolidge and family, 1924
Library of Congress, Reproduction #LC-USZ62-111377

Liberty, 1974
Gerald R. Ford Library

Susan, Mrs. Ford, and President Ford with Liberty and her puppies in 1974.
Gerald R. Ford Presidential Library

President Herbert Hoover, 1930
Library of Congress, Reproduction #LC-H824-T01-0224

President Lyndon B. Johnson speaks to the press while walking his dogs, Him and Her in 1964.
Lyndon Baines Johnson Library

President Ronald Reagan on a helicopter with his dog Lucky in his lap, 1985.
Ronald Reagan Presidential Library

BUDDY *written by:*

Kaitlyn

Christine

Kevin

Jacqueline

President Bill Clinton, 1995

Thousands of kids decided that President Bill Clinton needed their help! In December, 1997, letters poured into the White House suggesting names for the President's new puppy. It was quite a welcome for a squirmy three month old, chocolate Labrador!

The puppy was a gift from First Lady Hillary Clinton. She wanted the President to have a dog when their only child Chelsea left for college. Little did anyone know how important this First Dog would become to his owner.

The First Lady contacted Wild Goose Kennel in Federalsburg, Maryland. Mom, Sadie Rainbow Gold (a yellow Labrador) and Dad, Quantico's Stormy "Coco" Bear (a Chocolate Labrador), had a litter of nine pups, four girls and five boys. The owners, Linda and Richard Renfro, chose a chocolate-colored male and sent him to the White House without a name.

After hearing the kids' ideas, and thinking it over for a while, Clinton named the dog after someone important to him. Buddy was named for Clinton's great uncle, Henry Oren "Buddy" Grisham of Hope, Arkansas. Uncle Buddy was a dog trainer for 50 years and had died earlier that year.

Several weeks after Buddy arrived at the White House, the Monica

164

Presidential Dogs
by Skye Friedman

Lewinsky scandal hit the newspapers. President Clinton was accused of having an affair with a White House intern. Everyone was angry with President Clinton. "If you want a friend in Washington," President Harry Truman once said, "get a dog." Buddy fit the bill.

Buddy, playful and fun-loving, was totally loyal to Clinton, making sure he was always at the President's side. He went walking, fishing, and golfing with Clinton. The First Dog's favorite game was to tirelessly fetch a rubber ball.

Buddy was also an awesome diplomat. Everyone loved him, from the Secret Service Agents and the White House staff to the official guests. The only one who wasn't thrilled with Buddy was the First Cat, Socks. Their conflicts were popularized in the press, particularly Buddy's love of menacing his adversary. Socks didn't let himself get pushed around, instead the black cat usually stood his ground, bristling at Buddy's incessant barks. Before long, Buddy joined Socks as the most photographed pets in the country. In response to this wave of national good will, Hillary Clinton put together a book called *Dear Socks, Dear Buddy: Kids' Letters To The First Pets*. The letters included questions like, "I've heard that you're the first dog. Does this mean you have authority over the other dogs of the United States?"

When Bill Clinton completed his second term, Buddy accompanied the President on his farewell flight from the White House to New York. Buddy"'s tenure as a post-White House dog didn't last long. On January 2, 2004, Buddy was hit by a car and killed. The Clinton family was "deeply saddened" by Buddy's death. They issued a statement, saying that Buddy was "a loyal companion and brought us much joy. He will be truly missed."

Buddy was only four years old.

Buddy

CHECKERS written by:

| Jessica | Molly | Ariel | Emily | Kelli |

Does anyone know that a dog saved President Richard Nixon's career? Without his faithful Checkers, Nixon might not have been elected Vice President, or later, President. He might have remained a Senator or eventually become just a private citizen in California.

During his two terms in Congress, and a seat in the House Committee on Un-American Activities, Richard Nixon had built his reputation as an honest, flag-waving patriot. The young senator from California was selected by General Dwight Eisenhower as his Vice President running mate. In 1952, the famous campaign was underway when the news broke -- Nixon was not as red-white-and-blue as the country believed. Nixon's political career was in deep trouble. He was accused of political

corruption -- accepting thousands of dollars in "donations" to supplement his income. If the country believed the charges, Nixon would have been dropped from the ticket. A war hero such as General Dwight Eisenhower would never win the Presidency with a corrupt running mate.

During this period, the candidates and their families were constantly questioned by the media. Nixon's wife Pat had mentioned in a radio interview that their two daughters would love to have a dog. It wasn't long before Richard Nixon put the pieces together, reporting that

President Richard Nixon, 1972
Nixon Presidential Library

". . . we got a message from Union Station in Baltimore saying they had a package for us. We went down to get it. You know what it was? It was a little cocker spaniel dog in a crate . . . sent all the way from Texas,

166

black and white, spotted, and our little girl Tricia, the six year old, named it Checkers . . ."

Richard Nixon had to do something fast or the charges of political corruption would end his political career. Denying the accusations was not enough. He needed something fast, with national appeal, to distract the public from the negative attention. Checkers was perfect. To assert his innocence, Nixon claimed that the only gift he received was Checkers

Portrait
by Jessica Teves

. . . and you know, the kids, like all the kids love the dog. I just want to say this, right now, that regardless of what they say about it, we're going to keep it.

Who can resist dogs and kids? In this famous speech, later dubbed the "Checkers" speech, people across the nation bought Nixon's sincerity. After all, how bad can a dog lover be?

When Richard Nixon originally received Checkers he had no idea what he held in his hands. All he saw was a cocker spaniel. Checkers was not just any dog. He had a mission unknown to everyone until Richard Nixon's famous speech in 1952. Many people believe that without Checkers, Nixon would not have gotten elected.

Checkers' grave
Bide-A-Wee Memorial Park

Checkers lived with the Nixons until 1964, when he died at the age of 13, four years before Nixon was elected President. Technically, Checkers was a *Vice* Presidential dog. He is buried in the Bide-A-Wee Pet Cemetery in Wantagh, New York. Checkers started out as a gift for children, and but ended up being a priceless gift for Richard Nixon. Without Checkers, Richard Nixon would not have been such an important part of history.

167

FALA written by:

Carla

Adam

Alyssa

Matt

President Franklin Delano Roosevelt was furious. Stories were circulating that his dog, Fala, had cost the American people millions of dollars. It was 1944, and someone spread the rumor that Fala, the President's Scottish terrier had been left behind on the Aleutian Islands. Supposedly FDR sent a destroyer to find the dog, costing taxpayers millions of dollars.

In a speech to the Teamsters Union, President Roosevelt refused to tolerate the attacks on his beloved Fala.

"I am accustomed to hearing malicious falsehoods about myself," FDR explained. "Fala was not used to it, and his "Scotch soul was furious." The President continued to describe his outrage.

President Franklin D. Roosevelt, 1947
Library of Congress
Reproduction #LC-USZ62-87317

These Republican leaders have not been content with attacks on me, or my wife, or on my sons. No, not content with that, they now include my little dog, Fala . . . I think I have a right to resent, to object to libelous statements about my dog.

The famous Fala was born on April 7, 1940. As a Scottish terrier, he had a heavy-set body, short legs, and a long head with tiny upright ears. From the moment he went to live in the White House, Fala was the

President's best friend. It was said that the little dog went everywhere with FDR, except to Yalta when the President met with Stalin and Churchill to discuss the future of the post-war world.

President Roosevelt with Fala
Franklin D. Roosevelt Presidential Library

Anyone who came to the White House met Fala. He entertained many guests with his funny tricks such as rolling over, jumping, flopping around like a fish, and making a strange doggie smile. Fala spent every possible minute at FDR's side. Each morning the President had a dog bone sent up with his breakfast tray. In the evening, Fala would get a full dinner served to him, whenever possible, by FDR.

"Many times, I remember dignitaries and other important folks waiting for their supper until Mr. Roosevelt finished feeding Fala,"said Fred D. Fair, the President's Porter.

Fala traveled with the President on many trips, hopping on trains, cars, and boats. The little Scottie met many famous people including Mexican President Camacho and Prime Minister Winston Churchill. Fala was a constant companion to the President.

Portrait of Fala
by Carla Scolieri

In 1945, President Roosevelt died. Fala rode the President's funeral train and attended the burial services. After each gun salute, Fala barked and rolled over on the grass, performing the President's favorite trick.

Fala went to live with the President's wife, Eleanor Roosevelt. They got along very well, but Fala never forgot the bond between him and FDR. Every time Fala heard sirens he would perk up, as if the President was about to walk into the house. He always slept near the dining room door so he could watch both entrances, waiting for FDR to return.

Fala died in 1952 and was buried in the Rose Garden, near President Roosevelt, at Hyde Park, New York. At the FDR Memorial in Washington DC, there is a bronze statue of the President, with Fala by his side.

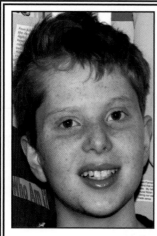

I remember my great-grandfather used to talk about a Scottish terrier named Fala. President Franklin D. Roosevelt had this dog for 12 years. My great-grandfather said that Fala was always at Roosevelt's side. He thought Roosevelt was a great President, and Fala was his faithful companion.

My great-grandfather told me that Mr. Roosevelt had a very serious problem walking. He was hardly ever photographed in his wheelchair, but that was the main way he got around. Fala would ride in his lap as Roosevelt's aides rode him up and down the ramps of trains and other places.

I think that Franklin D. Roosevelt was one of the most beloved presidents ever. He showed much love and affection for his dog, and the people saw this image everyday. If somebody remembers a famous person and also remembers his dog it says a lot about the popularity of that pet. I think Fala was a great dog, and I would have liked to have known him when he was alive.

Adam Weingarten

President Franklin D. Roosevelt
playing with Fala in 1943.
Franklin D. Roosevelt Presidential Library

FDR's Presidential Firsts

First (and only) President to be elected to four terms in office.

First President to appear on black & white television when he opened the New York World's Fair on April 30, 1939.

First President to appoint a woman, Frances Perkins, to the cabinet (Secretary of Labor).

First President to fly in an airplane while in office (1943).

First President to have a presidential plane, nicknamed "The Flying Hotel." It was a Boeing 314 Clipper, the largest airplane at the time.

First President to appoint a black general in the Air Force, Benjamin O. Davis Jr. Davis led the Tuskegee Airmen during World War II.

First President to invite all of the members of the Electoral College to a Presidential Inauguration.

First President to set the precedent for a special Inauguration Day Worship Service, in 1933

G.W. BUSH *written by:*

| Denise | Patrick | Thalia | Jessica | Caitlan |

People frequently write online journals and blogs. It's not too often pets are given the opportunity to share their daily lives on the internet.

Of course, if a pet just happens to be a White House legend, then the rest is no surprise.

Spot stands by herself in White House history. The brown-and-white springer spaniel was the only pet to live in the White House during *two* different administrations. Her mom was the beloved Millie, owned by President George H. Bush and First Lady Barbara. On March 17, 1989 Millie gave birth to a litter of puppies. The President's son, George "Dubya" and his wife adopted one

President George W. Bush, 2003

of the puppies and named her Spot.

When "Dubya" won the election in 2000, Spot returned to the White House with the new tenants. On her internet biography, Spot reported

One day my owners put me on a plane and took me to a huge white house with many rooms to explore. As I searched the house looking for tennis balls and bones, I was surprised at how familiar the place smelled. It was as if I had been there before.

I nudged my owner, President Bush, on the ankle and he said to me,

Portrait of Barney
by Caitlan O'Shea

"well, Spotty, how does it feel to be living again in the same house where you were born?"

Eleven-year old Spot was soon joined by Barney, a lovable, playful bundle of black fur. Barney was a gift from then-Governor of New Jersey, Christie Whitman. He was 12 weeks old and made instant friends with Spot. Both dogs had little to do with the reclusive First Cat named Willy.

President Bush with Barney.

Spot and Barney always greeted the President when he came home. Climbing into helicopters or Air Force One, the dogs often traveled with the Bush family to Texas or Camp David. Although it was sometimes difficult for Spot to keep up with his younger pal, the two dogs loved playing. Barney was quickest at chasing golf balls into holes or pushing a soccer ball with his nose. They were really good times for the Presidential Pups. Sadly, Spot died early in 2004, when she was 15 years old, leaving Barney as the only dog in the White House.

Meanwhile, Barney had become a media star. He appeared in numerous photographs with the Bushes and visiting political leaders. Barney had a high-tech interactive website, starred in his own "films," and answered e-mail questions from kids around the world. His opinion received international acclaim when *The Washington Post* reported an intriguing conversation on election night, 2004.

Portrait of Spot
by Caitlan O'Shea

With cameras crowded into his West Sitting Hall on the White House's rarely visited second floor, Bush broke the ice by asking Barney, the family's Scottish terrier, if he had anything to say about the events of the evening! Barney had no comment.

Shortly after, President Bush announced that he was giving First Lady Laura Bush a Scottish Terrier puppy for her 58th birthday. Miss Beazley moved into the White House, under the glare of media attention.

173

LADDIE BOY *written by:*

| Joe | Alyssa | Brittany | Stacy | Thomas |

Airedale Terrier

The White House was throwing a birthday party for dogs. Furry, four legged guests were invited to celebrate the birthday of Laddie Boy, and eat a very unusual cake. President Warren G. Harding, the 29th President of the United States, supported the strange festivities that honored his very popular dog.

Laddie Boy was born on July 25, 1919. He was an airedale terrier, a descendant of dogs brought from England in the early 1880's. Airedales were used during World War I and became popular war heroes. By the early 1920's, airedale terriers were the most popular breed in the country. Today they are known as the "King of Terriers."

Warren G. Harding worked as a newspaper publisher for many years. He started his career by purchasing a four-page newspaper in Marion, Ohio. He liked the business and stayed with it until he entered politics many years later. When the American people became tired of the post-World War I economic struggles, Warren G. Harding ran for the presidency on a campaign theme of "Back to Normalcy." He won the 1920 election. Little did anyone know how far that was from the truth. As soon as Harding took office, his administration was filled with scandals. Harding's reputation plummeted. One of the

Portrait of Laddie Boy
by Stacy Berkowitz

few things that made him look good was his beloved airedale terrier, Laddie Boy. Poking fun at Harding, while complimenting his dog, *The Washington Star* reported that "the White House has gone to the dogs."

Laddie Boy greeting the President and First Lady at the White House, 1923.
Library of Congress
Reproduction #LC-USZ62-132168

Everyone loved Harding's gentle presidential pup. The airedale earned a well-deserved "impeccable reputation," quickly winning the hearts and imagination of the country. The press made more fuss over Laddie Boy than Harding! In 1921, *The Washington Star* "interviewed" Laddie Boy, reporting the dog's opinion on everything from the members of the Presidential Cabinet to advocating for an eight-hour work day for guard dogs.

While Harding took advantage of Laddie Boy's popularity with the press, he really did love his dog. They had a very close bond. Harding showed this over and over again, making sure that Laddie Boy was always with him. Tales of Laddie Boy's amazing behavior were everywhere. People talked about how the airedale retrieved the President's newspaper every day, and fetched golf balls on the White House Lawn. Laddie Boy was known to hang out on the White House steps, greeting official visitors.

President Harding appreciated Laddie Boy's loyalty so much that he got him a hand-carved chair so the dog could sit in on cabinet meetings. The airedale must have been very patient to be able to sit still at such long, boring sessions! Harding even celebrated Laddie Boy's birthdays. On his

Laddie Boy and the First Lady
by Alyssa Slater

third birthday, Laddie Boy was presented with a large square cake made entirely from dog biscuits. Many other dogs were invited to the celebration. That must have been quite a sight, especially when all the "guests" finished their cake. Laddie Boy was in his glory.

When Harding got sick, Laddie Boy was thousands of miles away, but sensed something was very wrong. It was reported that the airedale tried to warn everyone by howling for three full days before the President died. In his three years in office, Harding failed to become a successful President. In those same three years, Laddie Boy became one of the country's most beloved pets.

While there have been many questions about Harding, his scandalous administration, and what exactly caused his death, no one ever doubted Laddie Boy. When Laddie Boy died, newsboys all over the country donated 19,134 pennies. The pennies were melted down and molded into a statue to honor the beloved airedale's memory. The statue is still on public display in the Smithsonian Museum, in Washington DC.

President Harding and Laddie Boy
by Thomas Burzynski

Laddie Boy's White House Scrapbook

In the absence of President and Mrs. Harding, Laddie Boy acted as host for the many children who rolled eggs on the White House Lawn, 1923.
Library of Congress, Reproduction #LC-USZ62-131868

Laddie Boy portrait, ca. 1920-1923
Library of Congress
Reproduction #LC-USZ62-121760

Laddie Boy and his portrait in silver, 1922
Library of Congress
Reproduction #LC-USZ62-131900

Laddie Boy greeting the President on his return from Florida, 1922.
Library of Congress
Reproduction #LC-USZ62-132064

SKIP written by:

Rachel   **Metin**   **Thomas**   **Maria**

Visitors to the White House couldn't believe their eyes as they watched a tiny dog riding all alone on a horse. It was a funny sight, and happened often with President Theodore Roosevelt's dog Skip.

Skip was a rat terrier, a new breed popularized by President Roosevelt. Skip had a short, hard blonde coat, and was only 18 inches tall. Skip's size made it hard to keep up with the horses. One day when the President was riding a horse, he saw Skip behind him, struggling to catch up. Roosevelt stopped to give Skip the chance to hop on the horse's back. Skip seemed to enjoy riding and did it more often.Before anyone knew it, Skip had learned how to ride the horse alone.

Theodore Roosevelt, 1900
Library of Congress
Reproduction #LC-USZ62-115917

Skip had a lopsided figure -- a wide body, short legs, hound-like nose, and terrier ears.

Actually, rat terriers were a mix of various terrier breeds, with Italian greyhound and beagles added along the way. Roosevelt described the small dog as cunning, fun, lively, and good to his family. Skip never left the President alone.

Skip had a lot of spunk and spirit. He met the President every morning at breakfast, standing up with his paws on Roosevelt's lap. When Roosevelt read a book, Skip settled into his lap. Most of all, Skip loved

Rat Terrier

178

to go to Oyster Bay, New York, with his beloved owner.

Although Skip was his favorite pet, Roosevelt had a lot of pets living in his White House, including a garter snake named Emily Spinach, a pony named Algonquin, and Eli, the macaw. The President, nicknamed Teddy, was well known for his love of animals and the outdoors. In 1902, Roosevelt was out hunting, a very popular sport in those days. There was no game, so his companions captured a bear for him to shoot. Roosevelt saw the helpless, captured bear and refused to fire at it. Word spread quickly about the President's act of mercy.

Storeowners living in Brooklyn, New York, decided to make a stuffed bear to honor Roosevelt. They put it in the window of their candy store and called it Teddy's bear. The rest is history.

It's no surprise that Teddy's bear quickly became a national craze, and is still going strong today. Teddy Roosevelt was a popular, versatile president who was well known for claiming that "no man has had a happier life than I have led; a happier life in every way." He was known for a myriad of accomplishments, ranging from writing, history, the military, and, of course, politics.

Just one year before Roosevelt left office, Skip died. The President sadly watched his beloved dog buried on the White House grounds. When Roosevelt finished his second term, his wife had Skip's body moved to the family estate at Sagamore Hill, New York.

"Teddy couldn't bear to leave him there," she said of the White House gravesite, "beneath the eyes of Presidents who might care nothing for the little mutt dog."

A Man of the People

In addition to being Vice President and President of the United States, Teddy Roosevelt held a wide variety of offices that demonstrated his intelligence, sense of adventure, and commitment to public service:
Deputy Sheriff in Dakota Territory
Lieutenant Colonel of the Rough Riders in the Spanish-American War
Police Commissioner of New York City
New York State Assemblyman
Governor of New York State
U.S. Civil Service Commissioner
U.S. Assistant Secretary of the Navy

Paws In Time

What does a clean-cut working dog like Gizmo have in common with a snarling gray wolf? Like Gizmo, most of us have wild, untamed members lurking in our families. Gizmo's most immediate relatives are Australian labradoodles. He is a purebred "designer mutt" with Labrador retriever and standard poodle in his ancestry. His roots, like all dogs, can be traced back about 150,000 years to the snarling gray wolf. In fact, every dog, whether it looks like Gizmo, a great Dane, or a Mexican hairless dog, has the same wolf blood. Although it is difficult to imagine, all dogs are related to one another.

Some experts believe that dogs split from wolves about 135,000 years ago, evolving into a separate population. How and when dogs became man's best friend is hotly debated.

There is an old cave painting that dates back more than 50,000 years. Many people have seen its "dog-like" animal, hunting alongside men. However, most experts argue that dogs were domesticated only within the last 15,000 years. Although experts may not agree on the time frame, most of them do agree that the first domesticated animal to join the human ranks was the dog.

Why, with all the animals roaming the world, did people choose dogs? Perhaps they didn't. Anyone who owns, visits, or otherwise loves dogs would probably agree that it worked the other way -- dogs chose people. Dr. Brian Hare and his colleagues from Harvard conducted a study that sheds some light on this puzzle. They found that dogs have a special skill that enables them to pick up on human cues. For example, a chimpanzee, who has greater intelligence than a dog, might notice that a person is looking at a box, but never get the hint that there's food inside. A dog would get the picture immediately.

Dr. Ray Coppinger, a dog behavior expert at Hampshire College, suggests that that it was "natural selection" that led to dogs domesticating themselves. They hung around campsites for scraps from human dinners, and the ones that learned not to be afraid survived, and flourished. The ones that couldn't be tamed simply died off. It makes sense, as dogs could have really helped the ancient hunter/gatherer people in many different ways.

Whatever their exact origin, dogs became an important part of human civilization. They have been found in sculptures and pottery of ancient Assyria, Egypt, and Greece. Homer, the Greek author of the Odyssey, wrote about dogs in the 9th century B.C. The ancient Romans relied on watchdogs and war dogs. Archeologists have found dogs in The Han Dynasty in China, which began in the 3rd century BC. At some point, people discovered that they didn't have to wait for natural selection (evolution) to get the dogs they wanted. Artificial selection, or dog breeding, worked a lot faster.

Hunting dog
Library of Congress LOT 12682 No. 12

Even the noblest purebred, like the royal corgis, could be bred with the scruffiest stray mutt, and there would be puppies. People may not be happy with how those puppies look or act, but they're still dogs. It just wouldn't work breeding a cow with a cat, or a monkey with a mouse, to bring about certain qualities! People are people, cows are cows, and dogs -- with their seemingly endless variety of features -- are all still dogs.

Dog breeding has been going on for centuries - leading to the amazing variety of size, height, weight, coat, color, and temperament that we see today. Dogs were bred to fit specific jobs, usually hunting, herding, guarding, tracking, and giving warning signals. In contrast, breed histories and pedigrees are fairly recent, beginning in the 19th century with the first kennel

Seventh annual dog show of the Washington Kennel Club, 1920
Library of Congress, Reproduction #LC-USZ62-124437

clubs. The world's first dog show took place in Great Britain in 1859 and the AKC (American Kennel Club) wasn't organized until 1884 -- making them all the new kids on the block when it comes to dog history.

It was not long before people got into the business of dog breeding, choosing to breed for the appearance of the dog rather than health or function. Responsible breeders work very hard to avoid the pitfalls of genetic disorders, while irresponsible dabblers perpetuate widespread problems through ignorance and profit motives. Consequently, many purebreds now come at risk with a host of genetic diseases and conditions. The notorious American puppy mills exacerbated the issues by recklessly breeding and inbreeding animals for pure profit, creating physical, psychological, and medical conditions that unsuspecting people can not imagine. Often there is heartache for families who unknowingly adopt pets with such

Gizmo

medical problems.

Today, the best place to get a purebred dog is from a responsible breeder. The second best place is from a shelter or rescue group that does not offer puppy mill rejects. Many people argue that the safest pets are hybrids, or mixed breeds, because their chances of inheriting a genetic disorder is greatly decreased. As you will see throughout this book, the mixed breed dogs, many from local shelters and rescue groups, make wonderful pets and working dogs. When you consider that millions of dogs enter shelters every year, there is definitely a "treasure" anxiously waiting to become part of your family.

As a designer mutt, Gizmo fits into a new category which attempts to get the best of everything. Kenneth Miller writes in LIFE the "Doodle may simply be the latest chapter in the continuing evolution of man's best friend. Rather than being bred for hunting or herding, dogs are now selected for traits that make them lovable members of the family -- who don't cause sneezing [allergic] fits. But when we tinker with living things, the results are never predictable."

That may certainly be true. Just look into Gizmo's eyes and maybe you'll catch a little bit of that old gray wolf -- then again, it may be long gone.

Chezster, a pomshi (pomeranian/shih tzu designer mutt) lives with the LaPorta Family

Coco, a labradoodle, Gizmo's sister

DeTAILS

Fascinating Canine Facts

*The Irish wolfhound is the tallest breed of dog at 32 to 34 inches high, while the English mastiff and the St. Bernard are the heaviest breeds (some grow to 220 pounds!).

*The Chihuahua is presently considered the smallest breed, weighing less than six pounds. However, the new "toy" and "teacup" dogs are coming in even smaller!

*The fastest breed is the greyhound, which can run up to 45 miles per hour on a race track.

*In a vote of 7500 people, Fala was voted one of the top ten dogs of the 20th century.

*Some of the oldest breeds still around today are: the Australian dingo, basenji, Canaan dog, saluki, chow chow,, shar pei, and akita.

*The most popular names for dogs in the United States and Australia are Max for males, and Jessie, Maggie, and Molly for females.

*Dogs are not color blind.

*Dogs perspire through their tongues, and the pads of

their paws.

*The chow chow has a black tongue.

*While all dogs look different, they have identical anatomy.

*Puppies are born helpless. They are blind, deaf and can't stand. They sleep 90 percent of the day, and spend the rest of the time nursing.

*Small dogs live longer than large dogs.

*6 to 8 million dogs enter pet shelters each year.

*A fertile dog can produce two litters of puppies each year. The average number of puppies per litter is six to ten.

*The first commercial pet food was a dog biscuit introduced in England, 1860.

*Dogs have twice as many muscles for moving their ears as people.

*Dogs that chase cars have learned that cars "run away." As a result, each time a dog gives chases, he "wins" and the behavior is reinforced.

*Dogs that turn in circles before lying down are mimicking an instinct from the wild that turns long grass into a comfortable bed.

*Twenty percent of pet dogs were adopted from a shelter.

Paw Prints On The Web

American Kennel Club www.akc.org
Americans With Disabilities Act
   www.usdoj.gov/crt/ada/adahom1.htm
ASPCA www.aspca.org
Assistance Dog Club of Puget Sound www.dogsaver.org/adc
Bide-A-Wee www.bideawee.org
DelMonte Foods www.delmonte.com
Delta Society www.deltasociety.org
Franklin D. Roosevelt Presidential Library
   www.fdrlibrary.marist.edu
FutureCorps
   www.newsday.com/other/education/ny-fc_home_page.htmlstory
Gerald R. Ford Presidential Library
   www.fordlibrarymuseum.gov
Gracie Foundation www.threedog.com/pawticulars/gracie.shtml
Guide Dog Foundation www.guidedog.org
Guide Dogs For The Blind www.guidedogs.com
Humane Society of the United States www.hsus.org
Iditarod Official Site www.iditarod.com

International Labradoodle Association www.ilainc.com
Kibbles 'n Bits www.kibblesnbits.com
Lewis & Clark Expedition www.lewis-clark.org
Long Island Petfinders www.longislanddogs.petfinder.com
Lyndon Baines Johnson Presidential Library
   www.lbjlib.utexas.edu
Newsday www.newsday.com
Pedigree's PAWS TO RECOGNIZE www.pedigree.com/vote
PetCo www.petco.com
Petfinders www.petfinder.com
Richard Nixon Presidential Library
   www.nixon.archives.gov/index.php
Rin Tin Tin ARFkids www.arfkids.com
Rin Tin Tin, Inc. www.rintintin.com
Ronald Reagan Presidential Library www.reagan.utexas.edu
Rutland Manor Labradoodle Breeding and Research Center
   www.rutlandmanor.com
Scout Dog Pages (Charlie Cargo) www.scoutdogpages.com
Smithsonian www.si.edu
The Scoop www.dogsinthenews.com
Therapy Dogs International www.tdi-dog.org
Three Dog Bakery www.threedog.com
Town of Babylon Animal Shelter
   www.townofbabylon.com/pets.cfm
U.S. Coast Guard Patrol Dogs
   www.uscg.mil/hq/g-cp/history/Beach_Patrol_Photo_Index.html
U.S. Customs & Border Protection www.cbp.gov
U.S. Department of Homeland Security www.dhs.gov
Viet Nam Dog Handlers Association www.vdhaonline.org
Viewpoints Photography www.viewpointphotography.com
Waggin' Wear www.wagginwear.com
Walmart www.walmart.com
White House Pets www.whitehouse.gov/kids
William J. Clinton Presidential Library www.clintonlibrary.gov

Canine Art Gallery

by Brandon Piskin

by Dean Simms-Elias

by Caitlan O'Shea

by Brian Demmett

by Maria Pokorny

by Patrick Goldberg

by Emily Bernstein

Meet The Heroes of Book Web!

Dr. Jeri Fink   Mrs. Donna Paltrowitz

Jeri Fink and Donna Paltrowitz are long-time friends and colleagues, who have collaborated on numerous projects. Together, they developed many series, including *Books By Kids, Books By Teens, You Are The Author!, Kids Take Action,* and *The Gizmo Tales.* They believe that young people should be active participants in the reading and writing of their own literature.

Dr. Fink is a family therapist, journalist, and author of many books for children and adults.

Mrs. Paltrowitz is an educator who has co-authored more than 60 children's books and software programs. They are neighbors in Bellmore, New York, living with their respective families, cats, Gizmo, and Coco.

Gizmo Tales For The Whole Family!

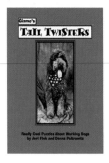

Check Out Gizmo's Mysteries

Corey's Web Unleashed

When evil things happen to the dogs in town, Corey and Gizmo go to work.
Ages: 8-12

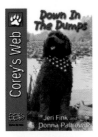
Corey's Web: Down In The Dumps

Corey and Gizmo dig for clues in the ghosts and garbage of Meadow Pond.
Ages: 8-12

Matthew's Tangled Trails

Matthew and Gizmo chase the cybercrook behind a bone-chilling scam.
Ages: 12-16

Don't miss our exciting BOOKS BY TEENS!

To Order Books or programs go to:

www.bookwebpublishing.com

or contact:

Book Web Publishing, Ltd.

PO Box 81, Bellmore, NY, 11710

NOTES

NOTES

NOTES

NOTES